Y0-EMQ-919

Beginning

Jerry Tiff

Outskirts Press, Inc.
Denver, Colorado

Chapter 1

"Bob"

The night was hot and humid. In the better parts of the city, air conditioners were grinding away in window frames trying their best to take away the heat. Some evaporators froze up from the humidity surrounding them, insulating the cold aluminum fins from the air, and stopping the cool airflow into the respective bedrooms. Irate and unknowledgeable owners flailed away at the machines with insults and blows, and slept fitfully on damp, tangled sheets.

Bob's sleep was unobstructed by failing air conditioners, or sheets wet with sweat. He and a pair of much older men were the only residents of a blind alley a couple of blocks North of the warehouse section of the old downtown, an area that twenty or thirty years ago had held viable small businesses. The businesses were gone. The buildings were considered run down ten years ago. The current residents were street people who lived out of sight in the rat-infested boxes in the alleys. Tonight Bob slept with his head against the cool cobblestones. A pair of older men shared the flattened wooden crate at the alley's dead end, their inebriated snoring resounding off the brick walls around them.

Bob was only vaguely aware of the tape pushed against his mouth, and the firm hands that grabbed his arms, lifting him to his feet. It might have been just another dream. "Yea, it's only another hazy dream. Everything is cool! I'm just fine."

They forced him from the dark alley and roughly tossed him into the back seat of the near new gray Ford sedan. Two of them jammed in beside him, while the third jumped behind the steering wheel and quietly pulled away onto the deserted, dimly lit street.

He had been under surveillance for some time. They knew he was shooting a lot of heroin. They also knew that he turned tricks to keep himself comfortable. He had a lot of regulars, a lot! He was perfect.

The Ford slowed, entered a short driveway, and stopped under the yellow glow of the single lamp that lit the large side door to the warehouse. The driver got out of the car, unlatched and opened the door, swung back behind the steering wheel, and drove into the huge empty building. The headlights illuminated an enclosed office at one end. They also illuminated a small Airstream trailer parked near the office. A large electric cord ran from the trailer to a receptacle on the wall of the office.

Without speaking, the two men in the backseat took Bob from the car up to the trailer, where the driver unlocked the door, and turned on a table lamp. One of the men hit his shoulder against the doorjamb as he pulled Bob inside. He swore as he and his partner took the staggering man between them into the bedroom. Bob was swung down onto the bed and fell into a heap as the men let go of him. "Yea, man this is some smooth dream. I'm cool. Shit man, I'm wasted!" He laughed to himself.

The driver prepared a syringe, mixed the white crystalline power with water in the tablespoon, and cooked it over the flame from the trailer's gas stove for a few seconds. One of the two men from the backseat rolled up the shirtsleeve covering Bob's right arm, produced a rubber tube and tourniqueted that arm. "Christ!" he said as he looked at the punch marks from the wrist to the elbow. He swabbed an un-pricked area where the vein stood nearly bright blue, with a cotton ball flooded with alcohol. The driver injected the syringe load of fluid, them removed the tourniquet, and tape from Bob's mouth. "Far out", he muttered as he drifted deeper into the rosy haze that spread over him as he spun slowly in golden softness on the nod.

Chapter 2

"Senate Bill 87788"

Senator Hillby, Democrat, had just provided the tie vote on Senate Bill 87788. In the Senate Gallery, Bill Hansen, ex-presidential Assistant For International Trade, and Satchel Green, ex-cabinet member slammed the arm rests of their seats, got up, and walked out. They knew what Senator Phillbroom, Democrat, would do with his vote, and that would be it!

"Our clients won't be happy with this one", said Green. Hansen threw him a brief glance as they walked quickly down the hallway. "Unhappy," Hansen thought to himself, "with all the money these guys tossed around, they're going to be fucking, big time furious! Someone is going to get hurt, hurt bad." Both men hurrying down the hallway could vaguely hear Senator Phillbroom's baritone voice, carried by speakers inside the gallery, as he started his oration on his way toward delivering the deciding vote. The Bill would pass.

They returned to their office after a rather long lunch. Their office manager, the telephone in her ear, looked up from the fully lit up phone board gave a fake sigh of relief, as the two men came in through the doorway. Covering the mouthpiece, she said in her normal dry tone, "The you know what has really hit the fan! I take it you two aren't back yet?" Green and Hansen shook their heads without smiling. "No Mr. Vevel. But, I expect them back soon. Yes sir, I'll certainly tell them. No Sir, I certainly won't. Yes sir I understand the urgency. Good day sir!" She cradled the handset, quickly picked it up again and pushed the hold button. The last outside line was now also tied up.

"I really think that you should start on this NOW," she said. "Bill, your voice mail is filled, and here is a list of those who said they hate voice mail and will only talk to you direct. Please note that the third name from the top on that list is Mr. Kogi."

"Thanks Gertrude," Hansen said with a slight bit of exasperation in his voice, as he read the list while walking to his office. "Welcome", she said, looking up at him over her Versace half-glasses. "And Satchel, here is your list. Ditto to Bill's situation", she smiled. "Only the names are changed." Satchel shot her a glance and half smiled at her subdued wit. As he passed Bill's office, Bill was already dialing the first phone number.

"This is Mary, Mr. Kogi's assistant, may I help you?" "Mary, this is William Hansen. I want to speak to Mr. Kogi, it's urgent and I am returning his call." "Mr. Hansen, he has just stepped into the Conference Room, please hold on. I'll get him for you immediately." In no more than a few seconds, a deep voice came on the line. "This is Kogi.

What happened up there this afternoon, Mr. Hansen?" Kogi's voice was quite abrupt. "Mr. Kogi, the two votes that we needed and believed we had, were swayed at the last minute. At the moment, I don't have the exact reasons for the betrayal, but I'm willing to bet that both Senators were somehow influenced by Senator Phillbroom. I will indeed investigate and report back to you." "I too will do some investigating and get back with you, Mr. Hansen. Please excuse me I must report to Tokyo. Good by." "Son of a bitch", Hansen yelled, after he slammed the phone down.

Green was busy on his phone as well. "No sir, we don't wish to make a statement at this time. We are evaluating options presented by passage of the Bill. As soon as we've made an analysis and worked up a statement, I'll call you. That's correct. Yes. By for now." Green walked into Hansen's office. "What was the yelling all about?" "That asshole Kogi is probably on the line with Tokyo at this very instant, grinding us up into little meatballs! This is what he has been waiting for. Meanwhile, I'm calling Senators Hillby and Cask to get their stories. This thing never should have happened, never. We've put so much industry in their respective states that they're having a hard time filling the jobs. And look at the fortunes we spent to get these clowns elected. It's undoubtedly Phillbroom's "Buy American" program that's responsible for icing us, but I told Kogi I'd investigate and I've got to get back to him with accurate information."

Hansen called both Senators, but could only get as far as their aids. Both told him that their respective Senator wasn't available, but would get back by phone before the day ended. Both aids were unnaturally tight, their voices giving posture to what Hansen presumed was their employer's up-to-the-minute attitude toward him. "Resoundingly fine start on your investigation Hansen", he said to himself, out loud. Then, "wait a minute, I'll call Phillbroom. Yes, I owe him congratulations for a battle well fought and won. Maybe his ego, and by now a couple of Jack Daniels doubles will have opened him up a little. What's to loose?"

Phillbroom's executive secretary answered the phone. Her voice and the racket in the background betrayed a party that sounded in full swing a few feet away from the phone. Hansen thought real fast, "hell yes, a party!" He feigned a wrong number, cradled the phone, and grabbed his jacket. The Senator's office was less than a five-minute walk away from his.

As soon as Hansen entered the building, he could have found the party room without knowing the floor or room. The music and laughter could be heard faintly even on the first floor at the Information/Security booth. Hansen showed his I.D., signed in, and took the elevator up one story. When the elevator door opened, he saw signs everywhere in the large hallway. "Buy American", they said, with small American flags making a border around the wording. Several of them had text added, "the job you save will be your own!" This was written with dark marker pen.

People were also everywhere, in the hallway, moving in and out of the open door to the Senator's office, and everyone seemed to have at least one drink in his or her hands. The sound was terrific, loud talking mixed with laughter, and punctuated by a five piece Dixieland Band chewing up, "There'll Be A Hot Time In The Old Town

Tonight." Hansen moved into the center of it all hoping to find Senator Phillbroom.

Hansen's forty-five year old, blonde good looks drew smiles from several handsome women as he passed by. Some of them knew him from his days with the President. Several looked at him as if they would like to know him. He offered his best public smile in return, making brief eye contact with each. "Where's Senator Phillbroom", he asked. "WHAT?" came the reply. "SENATOR PHILLBROOM, WHERE-IS-HE?" "FAR CORNER, WITH THE OTHER SENATORS." Hansen waved thanks and squeezed through the crowd. He was towering over a small group, gesturing with both hands as if trying to get a grip around an elephant, a huge grin on his face, spouting words in his Southern Drawl that could be heard even above the din of the room. There, in the group with drinks in their left hands, were the two Senators whose critical votes had decided the Bill's success, Senator Hillby and Senator Cask. The little group was decidedly gloating over the victory.

Senator Phillbroom saw Hansen making his way through to the little group, waved and shouted, "Billy, y'all come on over here." He bent a little and made a comment to the other five people who immediately half turned and smiled in Hansen's direction.

"Hi Harry," Hansen said as he joined the circle, and offered his hand to Phillbroom. "Great fight, Harry, and a good win." "Well Billy, it wasn't what you might call a miracle, but I guess my work was repaid. Hell son, you're standing there without a drink in your hand, let's us just remedy that." Phillbroom caught the arm of one of the catering staff and with a glowing smile on his face said, "Missy, will you please bring this young man what ever it is that he wants to drink?"

Hansen smiled at her, "A diet Coke, please." "Gentlemen, I think y'all know Bill Hansen," Phillbroom said. Hansen knew them as well, and shook hands all the way round. The smiles on both Hillby and Cask didn't change with eye contact. The good humor remained.

"Billy, I want to tell you that you also put up a pretty good fight out there, and I appreciate that kind of effort," said Phillbroom, "it's the American way!" His last three words were projected out into the crowd, and at least three-dozen people in close proximity cheered. Hansen felt a wave of exasperation rising which he hoped wasn't showing. The cheer added to the din in the room making it nearly overwhelming.

Hansen moved very close to Phillbroom and spoke into his ear, "I'd like to talk with you in private, I'll be brief." Phillbroom's smile never changed. "Sure son." "Be right back," he mouthed to the little circle. He put a firm hand on Hansen's left shoulder and steered him through the crowd, up to a locked door. He shuffled with a key ring, found the correct key and opened the door.

The room was a rosewood-paneled study; with a huge mahogany roll top desk, a two-person leather sofa, and an overstuffed easy chair. Everything in the room was expensive and in good taste. On one wall was a library of legal books. Against another wall was library table and four spindle back wooden chairs. Once the heavy door was closed, the room was quiet. "Have a seat Billy," Phillbroom said as he eased down into the easy chair. Hansen sat on the sofa. "Now, what can I do for you," Phillbroom fumbled in his pocket for a lighter that he used to fire off a Cuban cigar.

"Harry, I thought I had you beat out there today. I have busted my ass since the first of the year to defeat that bill of yours, yet when the vote went down you beat me. How did you do it? How did you ever get Hillby and Cask to turn their votes around?"

Phillbroom smiled, took a drag on the cigar, and slowly let the smoke out. The smile faded. He looked directly into Hansen's eyes. "Billy, you are a Lobbyist. I am a U. S. Senator. You have a point of view that's real and valuable. You represent a constituency, some of it mine, who want specific things to happen to better their position in this country. What those people, through you, propose is what has prevailed too much in the good old U. S. of A. It's killed our heavy industry in the past three decades, and threatens to make the little that's left disappear in the next five. My Bill, Bill 87788 requires any nation that wants to trade with us do it on an equal basis. If you want to sell cars over here, you have to let us sell a like number over there. If you want to sell farm goods over here, then, by God, you got to let us sell ours over there. Billy, it's time the people in this country got a fair shake overseas. The two senators you asked about just saw the light and voted the only honest way that they could. They voted to save this great country of ours."

Hansen went back to his office, unlocked the door, flipped on the lights, sat down at his computer, and started composing a report for Kogi. Phillbroom wouldn't tell him a thing. The two senators were unwilling to say anything as well. He would have to look elsewhere for answers. "Yeah, I have a feeling someone is going to get hurt bad on this one," he said to himself as he began to type. He thought for a second then picked up the phone. He would check with Satchel before he got too far on the report.

Chapter 3

"Circumstances"

Bob awakened. He had to pee badly. One of the men, who was left on guard, helped him up from the bed and steered him into the tiny bathroom. Relief was almost euphoric. He splashed the soiled rim with his wavering stream. Rivulets ran down the sides of the toilet. He didn't bother to shake off the last drip; he just put his cock back into his soiled underwear. Now to that wonderful soft bed. Just right now he couldn't remember the last time he had spent the whole night alone in a nice soft bed. In fact, remember is something he didn't do very much of anymore, either. An hour and a half later, they shot him up again. The small air conditioner on the trailer's top made the interior very comfortable. Out in the real world, the night was still hot and humid and a light rain had begun to fall.

Two of the men who had abducted Bob took the Ford to an "Open 24 Hours" donut shop. They bought a dozen frosted cake donuts and three large Styrofoam cups of coffee to go. "What the hell do these guys want with our junkie," one of them asked the other as they motored back.

"You got me. And besides, it ain't none of our business. We don't get paid for knowin' shit like that." "Well, he sure as hell is someone's business, idn't he?"

The silent alarm went off at the Page Resource Research Lab at three AM. Two patrol cars of the New Orleans Police Department arrived in less than two minutes and positioned themselves at opposite ends of the building. Two additional cars quietly stopped at the front door in less than three minutes time. All outside doors and windows were locked and closed. There was no apparent evidence of a break in. The manager's phone number was found, called, and he was there by four fifteen. Two officers went in first, with their side arms drawn. There was no one in the building. Initially nothing seemed out of place. The alarm was reset. That was how the reports would read.

The younger of the two men in the stolen, gray, Voyager van added another strip of packaging tape to the seal on the small Styrofoam box. The tape pulled at the tips of his thin rubber gloves when it touched them. "This shit makes me very, very nervous," he said to the driver.

"That stuff is about as secure as we can make it. In fact, you've indulged yourself in a little overkill, I'd say," came the driver's response, with a wiry smile. "I just don't want to get my ass kicked by this shit." "Relax, we'll have your package delivered in a few minutes, then you can wash your hands, take a shower, or frolic in the waves at the beach, if it will make you feel better. Your piece of this action could get you a month of first class treatment on Jamaica."

"Actually, my old lady has a bunch of relatives in Puerto Rico. I thought we might do a nice family visit while this heist cools out." "What the hay baby, we unload that shit in about fifteen minutes, we collect, and we're out a here. You can go the fuck to fucking Puerto Rico or wherever. I'm back in L.A. man, laying on Goddamn Venice Beach with the worlds finest pussy parading past my hard-on."

Ten minutes later the stolen Voyager was left, key in the ignition, engine running, at a curb, one block away from the drop point. At the drop point, dollars were exchanged for the small Styrofoam box. Then each of the three men involved went his separate way. The man with the Styrofoam box started toward a large black limo parked at the curb. He turned to see if the other men were watching, then crossed the deserted street, walked a block and a half, got into a small American sedan, and drove away toward the New Orleans downtown.

In a basement apartment in a three-story apartment building, the kitchenette was rigged with the necessary items to turn it into a miniature laboratory. The small Styrofoam box was handled with great care by a technician who obviously knew what he was doing. The tape seal was carefully penetrated by a fresh single edged razor blade. The two halves of the box were gently pried apart exposing the tightly closed test tube labeled, Page Resource Research Labs, #1044-8, Biohazard, HIV. On prepared culture dishes, he placed two drops of fluid from the test tube, placed the covers on each, and immediately moved them inside the incubator. Seeing that all was in progress, he made a phone call to a man he had never seen, and never would.

Hamilton's private line rang. He picked up the receiver. A voice said, "This is Mister Smith, your order is being processed. It will be available in five days." "Thank you Mister Smith, I'll take care of it." Our battle plan is unfolding nicely, Hamilton thought as he cradled the handset. "Onward Christian Soldiers, forward into battle," he said out loud quietly. His old soldiers stern expression never changing, he said to himself, "we will, in the name of God, take back our streets and our morality. This is the beginning. The Committee must then meet in five days. I shall remind them that this is a military action; therefore, ultimate discretion and security must prevail. This is war. The stakes are extremely high for everyone connected with its planning and implementation. They are all professionals, and now they must also be soldiers, Christian Soldiers. It never hurts to make one's position definitive and clear. They'll be a little bit more careful because of it," he thought, turning his attention to the other work laid out on his desk.

Chapter 4

"Kogi"

Kogi's network in the District of Columbia may not have been as large in the U.S.A. as the old KGB, but it was more efficient. Very little of what was going on in the nation, especially in Washington D.C. escaped the scrutiny of his organization, on a general basis. Trained manpower was available around the clock for whatever it was called upon to do. Information was task number one. When Kogi set the organization in motion, it got results.

The afternoon of the vote on Senate Bill 87788, Kogi set his organization the task of knowing about Senator Phillbroom. At the end of the first twenty-four hours nearly a half million bytes of information were on disk, including the reports from researchers, readers, Congressional specialists, and discreet surveillance teams. Insider information was provided by those who responded to orchestra tickets to "Cirque de Soleil" or forty-yard line seats for the Redskins, or people directly employed by Phillbroom but on Kogi's payroll. Kogi was provided with an annotated update twice daily. Complete information was available at a computer stroke. After the second day, enough information was on file to produce a nearly complete biography on the senator. Word was passed to zero in on the man's likes, dislikes, personal habits, and vices. Use utmost discretion. Don't arouse suspicion. Be subtle, detailed and accurate, just as you have been. We have plenty of time.

Kogi knew, before Hansen called him, what his report would contain. He knew Hansen had no answers. Kogi was however, beginning to find the answers to why votes were moved, but he certainly would not tell Hansen. Kogi felt no compunction to collaborate with Hansen. Hansen was, simply put, an outsider who had been paid to perform a task, and had failed at great expense. Kogi accepted Hansen's report with reserve and politely told him to keep on with the investigation. After all, the contract between their respective firms would terminate on the first of the year. Hansen may as well be kept at a task. Perhaps one that he could handle, thought Kogi.

Kogi had all the data in place and available for whatever countermeasures the home organization wished to initiate against Phillbroom's Bill 87788. This, even though it was understood that the president would indeed sign it when it came out of the House. The fact remained, that he hadn't signed it yet. There was absolutely no question that they would stand still and meekly let it happen. Kogi guessed, privately, that several moves would be made. Some would be subtle; some would be something less than subtle. An of course some would be made to mislead or confuse whomever might be watching the plan develop, if the situation called for it.

Chapter 5

"Twelve Months Prior To The Vote On Bill 87788"

Hamilton's workday never ended at five or six when the last of his flextime employees accelerated out of the parking lot. There was always this or that detail that could do with resolving. And if one were to ask why he didn't call it a day, the answer was really quite simple. He enjoyed being the only one in the building. The building belonged to him. He had created his business with his own hands and mind. He could reach out and touch the desks, the chairs, and the computer terminals that caused people to be employed. Tonight one hundred families ate well together because of his employment. That pleased him. Alone in his building, he could still feel the presence of their ambitions, their dreams for the future. He could sense, even in their absence, the energy and dynamics of their presence still flowing throughout the workplace. Hamilton could detect their energy mixing with his, their strengths combining with his, the geometric generation of ideas, solutions, and innovative invention. It was overwhelmingly exciting. And he was the spark that ignited it every day.

Hamilton, without question, loved his business creation. His love allowed him to tolerate, to a point, the governmental bureaucracies that fed off of it. When their mask was pulled down their only contribution was to perpetuate themselves, regardless of the agency or name on a door or glowing pronouncement on their behalf by some selected or elected politician. When things needed doing, they were done by a guy out there with the spark, not by a bureaucrat or politician who jumped on the bandwagon after the fact.

Things did indeed need doing, right now. Hamilton saw the nearly overwhelming need. Too many things were out of proportion. There were already too many people, and those people were pumping out too many babies. There was too much lawlessness, and too many laws and lawyers. People were by and large not willing to accept responsibility for their own action, perpetuating an ever-growing circle of greater governmental intervention to take the place of personal responsibility and enterprise. Hamilton would take the responsibility, he had had enough.

Twenty plus years of military life had implanted a respect for discipline. Command experience had emphasized responsibility. He was solidly grounded in both, and held an open distain for those who weren't. Colonel Hamilton, after his second tour in Viet Nam, had also found Jesus again. It was during his second tour that the firebase he commanded was hit by a devastating mortar attack. He was flown out in critical condition. Twelve surgeries, a thousand prayers, and nearly two years later he took his first step with rebuilt legs. Jesus had seen him through.

Now it was payback time. His country needed him as never before. Law and order had broken down because of a faulty Judicial System that was bent more on it's own self-preservation and compensation than on serving Justice. Laws were created to perpetuate lawsuits, and replace individual responsibility. God's own laws, Hamilton thought, the Golden Rule, "An Eye For An Eye," were scoffed as being dated. Felons, who should have been done away with, were put back on the streets sometimes with just the equivalent of a hand slap. The "War On Drugs" was a farce, another government boondoggle, another pork barrel project. Drugs were more available than ever before. The streets were completely unsafe because of them. Homosexuality, drug addiction, theft, prostitution, muggings, kidnapping, drive by shootings, these and other crimes against this Christian nation were rampant, on the rise and the direct result of drugs, and liberalism. The country he loved was dying because of drugs and liberalism. He knew the answer. "Let them die by the sword."

He had casually led discussions on these problems with his Wednesday night prayer group, made up of several men and women of his own age and circumstances. Initially, there was some hesitance toward the subject matter, but gradually most of the group opened up and it appeared the majority believed the same as he did. Hamilton carefully and thoughtfully watched, then cultivated the more influential in the group. The chosen five met Thursday evenings in the comfortable surroundings of his library, in his home. At the same time, he fully developed his plan of attack. The plan was so simple. Once started, it perpetuated itself. The plan however, was not to be introduced to the group until after it was totally agreed that the content of the meetings would be kept secret.

Hamilton knew that it was not just his immediate city that was in need of repair, but the whole country needed cleansing. Why not cleanse the whole country? His plan would work in the immediate area. Why not take the cleansing nationwide? The difference would be simple logistics, that's all. A few more people would be involved, key people, nothing more. Why not a nation wide assault? He would be in command. It wouldn't be difficult. Jesus would see him through.

A few major cities throughout the country, places that were teeming with the vermin, would be where he would start, New York , Chicago, New Orleans, Atlanta, Los Angeles, and of course San Francisco. Begin the plan with a few major cities, and the rest of the country would take care of itself. The cleansing would spread outward from these key cities. Time was all that was needed after that.

Small task force groups would be formed in these major cities patterned after the one he would set up locally. They would set up fast, perform the tasks, and then disband. Guerrilla tactics! It would work perfectly. It would be the Lord's work.

Hamilton had chosen his committee of five well. When the plan was ultimately presented, there was robust endorsement. The questions that followed were supported, so no one questioned the intent. Only the logistics seemed of actual concern. And in respect, Hamilton was quick to show that indeed he had the answers. He asked that notes not be taken. Any dates or telephone numbers must be memorized, not written down. Again he emphasized the need for complete secrecy. "We must not let our zeal for God's work jeopardize that work," he said. "From this night on we are all involved in clandestine operations that if found out could have serious consequences for everyone in this room. Now for everyone's information, I am contacting a private detective whom I've known for a number of years and whom I've employed and found to be professional, dependable and quite discreet, who is available for projects such as ours. His contacts are likewise professional, dependable, and discreet. I can tell you that they do not come cheap but their work is guaranteed. It's true, these are not Christian men, however work such as this demands that we are expedient. Yes, it's true; we are at war with a non-Christian foe. However we must of necessity, as in any war, select allies of strategic importance, whom we feel best, fits our purposes. As to their identity, I think you'll agree the due to the covert nature of their work we will only refer to them as Beta Group."

"I have made city assignments to each of you. You will be working directly with them, the Beta Group, in each of the selected cities. Your responsibility will be to pattern a response team effort after what you'll see developed here in New Orleans. Each of you will spend about two weeks in his respective selected city at the task. We will be working with the same Beta Group members in each city. Their job will be basically as repetitive as each of us can make it."

"When each of you arrives at your respective city, you will establish yourself in a good hotel in the city center, one of your own choosing. This must have all the appearances of a bona fide business trip. You'll then report to me by phone on my private line only once unless you run into a problem that requires more assistance. No faxes, please, nothing written down. I will coordinate movement of the Beta Group to your assigned city. Once there it's your job to set up the scenario of their work. Get a rental car in order to scout the area. Turn it in every two or three days, and get one of a different color and make from a different company. Nothing flashy. Once the scouting is finished and you've made your selection, you'll ride with Beta Group to familiarize them with the subject. Your only direct contact with them after that will be to deliver the material that I'll provide. Beta will do their job, and advise you. You will advise me. Then you'll fly home."

Chapter 6

"Back To Real Time."

Hansen and Green pooled all of their sources and resources to put together the reasons for Senators Hillby and Cask turnabout votes. Predictably, they had sold out for political expediency. A Bill that they were writing to toughen immigration policy was nearly ready to present and naturally they were looking for primary support. Philbroom had made it quite clear about the hand washing business of politics and had promised his complete backing (which meant a minimum of forty per cent of the Senate at the moment). Hillby and Cask had no choice. On the surface Hillby and Cask made it quite clear that "Buy American" had turned their heads and hearts. Both had called Hansen the day after the vote and each had relayed his apology for the change, with nearly convincing candor. Later in the afternoon, both had gone on a Public Television News program waving the same banner. Phillbroom was certainly getting his monies worth. It was obvious that their interview had taken place at Phillbroom's Victory Headquarters with the Buy American posters behind them, but without the predatory females and the Dixieland jazz band doing their things. CNN and the major networks had done their obligatory blurb, and then quickly passed over the major ramifications of the Bill. Maximum airtime was twenty-eight seconds. Then, on they went to a story about a mother protesting fluoride in the drinking water. She claimed it had produced early puberty in her ten-year-old daughter, which lead to overt attention from the boys and pregnancy. Air time, eight minutes!

Kogi had scooped Hansen and Green by nearly six hours, finding the actual reason for Hillby and Cask's departure from the opposing side on the Bill. He immediately contacted the Tokyo Office, and had received confirmation for hiring activists in Washington, New York, and San Francisco in order to mount an immediate attack against the Bill. These people would be in front of TV cameras in time to make the five o'clock news. Their main theme would be the Congressional sell out to Big American Business at the expense of the American consumer. Kogi was willing to spend the additional retainer money for the attorneys. They would be needed when the pushing and shoving started, and bones and windows got broken. It would be program as usual for the rent-a-mob business!

Kogi was aware of where he was at all times. Now in particular, he saw a path that would take him toward the direction of his goal, besting the opposition in a promotional bout. He would create so much heat about this Bill 87788 that he'd have Phillbroom by the throat in three days and a revision Bill to counter it, up for a vote in three weeks, maybe less. Most certainly he would get enough fervor started in the press that the Bill would get killed in the House. Money was no object provided it got results. Kogi said, "Mary, please get the head of the House Foreign Affairs Committee on the phone. This is urgent. I must speak to him right now."

Chapter 7

"A Junky"

Bob awakened on the fifth morning in the travel trailer. His bladder was full again, but everything else was still in a haze. He made it to the toilet and back to the bed where he got his morning fix. He had no idea of how long he had been in this situation, but it was great. They had kept him well supplied with the shit, and even insisted that he shower. Food was available, and he would take a little once in a while, but the fixes were what he wanted most. These guys had plenty of heroin. It was pretty good quality China White, not that black Mexican stuff that was becoming more prevalent on the street. No one made any demands on him. There was no sex, no perversion, and no abuse, none of the usual things that made up his daily life. Bob wasn't sure what they had in mind but as long as they kept him high, hell, it didn't matter. He knew that when the time came he'd be available for what ever it was. He thought about asking, but then decided to keep his mouth shut, and just go with the flow. After all, life was pretty damned good at the moment.

It was well after dark when the driver brought the Ford into the warehouse. He pulled alongside the trailer, parked, got out with a small Styrofoam box and walked into the air-conditioned trailer. The cooled air hitting the back of his shirt made it icy where it had dampened with sweat. "I got the stuff for this big assed injection we're supposed to give him," he said to the two guards sitting, sipping beer, and playing Gin at the dinette. "We're soon out of this dump and on the road." " Man I'm bored stiff," one of them said, "it'll be just fine to get out of this goddamned trailer." The other one said, "Gin."

"Okay time to shoot up the junkie," said the first one. "Make sure you have fresh rubber gloves on this time. Oh yeah, we're supposed to use painter's facemasks when working around this stuff. So get 'em on. When you're both ready I'll load up."

Bob's life all of a sudden changed radically. The free junk, the soft sheeted bed, the comfortable surrounds were gone. He was back on the street. He couldn't understand it. They had just dumped him back on the street. No one said, "boo." They didn't even ask for a blowjob. They zoned him on some of that smooth shit they had, and he woke up back in his alley with ten bucks in his pocket, surrounded by the cardboard boxes he had lugged there a couple weeks ago. No, it just didn't figure. But something that did figure is he couldn't find his stash or his kit, in Fact, all of his stuff was gone. Some asshole must have taken it while he was at the trailer. It was going to take some fast action to get his hands on some cash before he started crashing. Time to find a couple of regulars or maybe hang out on the strip, wait for a player to find him. The regulars first, the sure cash now, he decided.

"Hey Michael, thought you might want a little fun this afternoon," Bob said into the payphone mouthpiece. "Sure, I'll be right over." Bob hung up the phone and fished in the coin return slot for non-existent returned change, then left the phone booth heading in the direction of his first one hundred bucks of the afternoon. His index finger and thumb encircled Mike's penis while the rest of the fingers held his scrotum. The penis was slightly bigger than when he first touched it. Bob pressed his index finger and thumb gently and firmly into the crotch, then gently squeezed the penis and held the pressure for several seconds. The cock visibly grew. Starting at it's tip, he slowly took it all in his mouth, pressing his lips to encircling thumb and finger accentuating the pressure at the base. Mike let out a gasp. Keeping pressure with his lips against the shaft, he began a rhythmic movement up and down. After the first three thrusts the penis was fully erect. In less than a minute Mike came as Bob finished him, the last ten seconds with a full hand grip. Mike's trembling legs gave out as he sank back against a table in the stockroom.

Bob now had enough for a single hit. Time to line up the shit. Later he could work the rest of his client list for the evening and morning supply. It would be good to build a little stash.

"Hey Bob, haven't seen you in a while. You get busted?" asked Lerouy, Bob's supplier.
"No man, I got lucky, " smiled Bob as he took the pass and headed in the direction of his new concealed kit. He was

beginning to get cotton mouthed and starting to feel sick, a flu kind of sick. It seemed like a month since he'd felt a need like this; maybe it was a week, or maybe a year, who the hell knows. Those guys with the trailer had really taken good care of him. "What was that all about anyway? What," he said out loud to himself.

Lerouy looked back over his shoulder. "You talkin' to me man?" Bob was too heavily into himself and too far away to hear Lerouy. All he could think about was heating that pea and getting it into his vein, like fast.

Chapter 8

"Off We Go"

The prompter light came on. The producer cued the talent who said, "Hi, this is Glenn Glege. This afternoon we're live here at University and Shattuck, in Berkeley, where a demonstration against the Senate passage of Bill 87788 is in progress. There must be at least a hundred people here. Some are carrying signs." The camera focuses in on a hand carried sign that reads, 'Big Business Collusion, higher prices for the little guy.' A loud bullhorn interrupted the sound of the talent's voice, "WHAT DO WE WANT? KILL THAT BILL." The reply came from the assembled group, "Kill That Bill."

The principal camera shot downward from above the talent, getting his bust shot and picking up a partial view of the man with the bullhorn. In the background cars slowly moved past, turning onto Shattuck or going forward down University. Some of the passengers hung out windows waving at the camera and giving peace signs with both hands. A couple managed to flip the bird before the cameraman became aware and zoomed in toward the front of the crowd. The talent said, "The bulk of those present are from a group calling themselves the Coalition for Lower Living Costs. I've just spoken to their leader Rendel Schultz. Mister Schultz told me that they want to see Senate Bill 87788 defeated because they believe it will contribute toward rising inflation, the loss of jobs, higher prices for consumer goods and they see the Bill as a sellout to big business at the expense of the working guy."

The talent begins to speak just as the bullhorn starts up again. Over the bullhorn he says, "More, later, on the six o'clock news." Kogi turned off the built in TV set with the remote and picked up his private phone and dialed. "This is Kogi," he said, speaking slowly into the mouthpiece. "I don't see enough passion in Berkeley. And after all, it is Berkeley." He placed the handset back on its cradle. The Previous three broadcasts had been to his liking. There had been a lot of signs moving up and down, fists shaking, shouting, and general animation that seemed to be lacking in the California scene. Word would be passed to Mr. Schultz in a matter of seconds. Kogi expected to see a better performance in an hour during the Bay Area six o'clock news.

The old Beechcraft C-45 flew straight and level at thirty-five hundred feet. The two Pratt and Whitney nine cylinder radial engines purred in stereo. Hansen had bought the airplane ten years ago with money he had made on hog futures. As a result, the plane was named "Pork Barrel One." The name had raised eyebrows where he lived, Washington, D.C. It was thought to be in bad taste by most of his friends who were of course, employed by the Federal Government. The painting of a pig looking out of a winged wooden keg graced the nose on either side below the cockpit windows. And, as period nose art went well with the restored military markings, circa nineteen forty-three. That was the year the plane was manufactured.

Maybe this was a lousy time to be flying around, but Hansen needed a little diversion. He needed to get away from direct confrontation with everyone and let his brain cool out. Flying had always given him that. It required the concentration that took him away from everyday things, forcing him to let go. It often changed his perception of a problem in a positive way. Today Satchel and Gertrude were minding the store. Nothing out of the ordinary was expected, so Hansen decided to play hooky, using the Beechcraft.

He had put together an hour and a half flight into a little grass strip near Nags Head. From the airstrip it was a short stroll through the dunes, to a nice section of nearly deserted beach. It was the right place to spend an afternoon thinking, or not thinking.

Over flying the runway to make sure it was clear, Hansen did the landing checklist after descending to twelve hundred feet and entering a standard traffic pattern on the downwind leg. With the prevailing wind straight down the runway, he made a magnificent and rare three-point landing.

With a couple of sandwiches in a brown bag, a paperback in one hand, and his trusty old stainless Thermos full of ice tea in the other, he opened the cabin door. A ten-knot wind greeted him as he swung down onto the airstrip's short Bermuda grass. The hot sun immediately began drying the perspiration from the back of Hansen's long sleeved khaki shirt. Just before closing up the airplane, he grabbed a rolled bamboo beach mat from its hiding place just aft of the door.

Very few feet had imprinted the pathway leading to the beach. Hansen smiled to himself at the thought. It was his secret getaway spot. The whole thought was made more delicious by the great weather. At the high place in the path he turned and gazed back at the Beechcraft. "God how I love that plane," he said out loud. The Beech had been a trusted friend, and one of a handful of friends who had survived the divorce seven years ago. He didn't want to calculate the year-to-year cost of maintaining this friend, but after all, he paid himself a good salary. He could afford the expense. And days like this one made the airplane's worth increase exponentially.

Muscles relaxed as the sun's heat penetrated the skin on his back, arms and legs. He lay face down on the mat. A dune deflected most of the wind, allowing only light zephyrs across his body. The sweat came fast. Hansen's existence boiled down to his warm skin, the sun, and the mat beneath him. The brain had switched off when his face touched the bamboo mat.

She came to him out of the sun. Her loose beige dress floated to the ground, revealing a beautiful tanned female body as she stepped slowly, one foot in front of the other, down the shaft of sunlight. Each step toward him primed her titillation. She had always loved him. She had always wanted him. She is going to have him now, on this beach, in this sunshine. The scent flowed over him from the Hibiscus flowers in her hair as she straddled him, knelt down and looked deeply into his eyes, poured love into him with her eyes, her smiling lips and tingling body. The sun was at such an angle that he could only see the outline of her face. He instinctually knew her, but couldn't recognize her. If only he could see her face. She began to lower herself onto his torso. The sun was still in his eyes. She came closer. Hansen brought his hand up to shade his eyes and asked, "Who are you?" He awakened with a start.

The seagull, scolding from atop the dune, squawked one more time then flew off toward the water. Hansen was awash with sweat, lying face up on the mat. It took a moment of adjustment from the dream to reality. He felt zapped. There was no one around, at least within sight, let alone a beautiful mysterious woman with wanton desires. The bulge in his Speedos testified to his connection with the content of the dream. "It's time for some ice tea."

Although now awake, nothing stayed around in his mind. Nothing would focus. The nap hadn't really refreshed him. It only made him groggy, a little languid. "Don't fight it. Give yourself a treat, stay mindless," he said to himself, grinning. A large swig directly from the Thermos nearly gave him a headache, it was so cold. With the third drink, his head began to clear. He sat up, and picked up the paperback book. Jimmy Buffett's writing always left him with a smile on his face, book or song, it didn't matter. This book, about a pilot wandering around the Caribbean, getting into and out of trouble, was perfect beach reading. Three hours flashed by.

It was hot inside the Beechcraft. Not a lot of air passed into the plane through the open cockpit side windows. Next time he'd leave the door open as well. After a brief pre-flight inspection, Hansen stepped onboard, pulled the step in after him, and closed the door. Sweat fell into his eyes as he hunched over, in the low headroom, walking up the aisle to the cockpit. As the airplane climbed, the flow of air through the Beechcraft's interior cooled the cockpit to a pleasant temperature. The plastic coated wheel, however, stayed hot to the touch for the next twenty miles.

Chapter 9

"Moving Right Along"

Hamilton's private line rang. "The last city on Beta Group's list has been completed. I'm coming in on the Delta red-eye, it arrives in New Orleans at two twenty-five tomorrow morning." "I'll see you then, next Thursday, at our regular meeting. Praise the Lord." "Praise the Lord," came the reply.

Hamilton smiled, and briefly made a mental note of the time and date. To himself he said, "Our work is now complete. The rest is in God's hands. Vengeance is mine, saith the Lord."

He felt relieved. The operation had gone without a hitch. Everyone had done very well. He would complement them at the meeting. Beta Group's fee was a little greater than he anticipated, originally, but they were paid in full in advance. Everything was paid except the travel costs of the task force groups involved. This he would pay, only if requested. They believed in the project, so why shouldn't they have a small stake in it via their trip expenses? He had drawn cash out of the business and from his personal accounts over the last three months that he knew would meet the expenses generated by the committee members. The total cost was his offering. He knew he would feel joyous when the last dollar was paid. He would then have done his part, lived up to his Christian responsibilities, used his expertise for the grace of his God. He had now given back to society. Soon the cleansing that he had begun would begin to have its effect. Soon, and forever!

Phillbroom sat his drink down, reached over, picked up the remote and clicked off the club's TV set. "Those assholes out in Berkeley, they don't know from nothin. Every time someone sneezes in this country, they are out there fifty deep, protesting it," he said to no one in particular, and just as his luncheon guest arrived.

In truth, this well financed, well thought out demonstration, was doing better this time, with respect to the choreography requested. The camera was held longer on the crowd. The crowd took their cue from the prompt light on the camera. With additional pushing and shoving, shaking of signs, and raised voices, the message came across the TV screen vivid and loud, "Kill the Bill." The PBS nightly news had chosen this scene to use in an update on Bill 87788. Phillbroom had been advised by a friend at WNET Boston that it was going to happen. Things might get tossed around a little in the House for show, but Phillbroom didn't see any reason to expect the Bill not to pass. His staff was doing a fine job lining up the votes. He had an extremely strong political presence. Pretty much nothing got done in Washington without his approval. This fact wasn't wasted by the staff in their efforts. And the Senator stayed informed of the progress. The vote was still about three weeks away. Things looked good.

Doug Sels, Head of the House Foreign Affairs Committee, pulled the lettuce and tomato salad closer to the edge of the table, and stabbed a complete fork full which he stuffed into his mouth, followed by a sip of the straight up martini. Sels talked with his mouth full. Phillbroom hated that. The man was always in too much of a hurry or he had no table etiquette. Possibly both. Phillbroom sat at a discrete distance, hopefully just beyond Sels chewed food range, and took a sip of his bourbon and water.

"Harry, I've had some calls, questioning this Bill of yours." Sels chewing didn't slow as he spoke. "Go on Doug."

"Some people don't know what to make of it. They're afraid the Mexicans will stop sending this lettuce up here in the wintertime, for one thing." Sels laughed, small particles of food flew through the air. Phillbroom moved his drink back on the pretext of being about to take a sip. "They're afraid the Canadians will stop sending down that Black Velvet. They seem to think that the price they're paying for Toyota four wheel drives is going to go up. They don't think we'll be able to sell the Russians a damned thing, 'cause they don't have anything we want, beyond some dancers and musicians. In short, they don't seem to think that it's very well thought out!"

"I'll tell you what, Doug, if you haven't done it yet, read that Bill. In fact, I'll make sure you get an extra copy. But read it, take a close look at it yourself. I think you'll see that this bill basically takes aim at protected foreign markets, and dumping of goods in the U.S. of A. Take a good close look at it. Then come back to me if you have any questions."

"To be perfectly honest, Harry, I haven't read your Bill. And, I haven't read the Bill being worked up by Clive Cording in the House either," he lied. "But, I promise I'll dig into both of them with equal vigor."

"I had heard that Cording was involved in a very softened up revision of my legislation," Phillbroom lied. "Let's get together the middle of next week again, for lunch, when we can discuss the merits of both these ideas."

"Done deal, Senator. Same time and place?" Sels asked, looking around the dark wood paneled dinning room of the Senator's club.

"Why yes, this little old place will do just fine. Meanwhile, tell me about your golf game, Doug. Word has it you stumbled into a hole-in-one last week."

"Things do get around in this town. Don't they? Well, yeah, that's the first time in twenty years of play for me."

Just before the entree arrived, Phillbroom excused himself and headed for the men's room. He scanned the room carefully before picking up the telephone, dialing and speaking. "I have to eat lunch with this clown to find this kind of thing out? What the hell am I paying you all this money for, just to pat me on the ass and tell me how right I always am? I don't care if you and that entire staff of yours has to work straight through the night, by tomorrow at eight

A.M. a complete report, and I do mean complete, on this Clive Cording thing will be on my desk. Is that clear? Damn it, I hate these kind of surprises."

Bob had turned enough tricks to just keep himself comfortable. He noticed that it was taking more than just the morning and afternoon hits to stay comfortable. Sometimes it took another half pea to get that rush he had felt before. After the really good shit the trailer guys had given him, it was definitely taking more money, in fact nearly twice the amount as before to keep high. And, the stuff he could score was nowhere near the quality of the trailer stuff. What it all amounted to was that he needed more money. He knew a few guys who hit on him to take it in the ass. And, he had a few times. They paid double the price of a blowjob. Once he had even done two guys at the same time. They had made him shower when he went up to their place, but most of his clients didn't need that, they just wanted to get off. But, the shower guys paid two hundred bucks. He needed more of that kind of dollar action, it made money the quickest. Sex was never a motivation for him. Somewhere along the way he had lost the need or the appetite for it. Now, it was just something he did that he got paid for. It was what he did.

"Look, if you want to do that kind of action," Lerouy told him, "you got to clean yourself up a bit. The crap you got for clothes don't turn nobody on. You a little too dirty, man. You mouth ain't seen no toothbrush fo' months, and the res' of you also ain't got no appeal. If you want to play in that league you got to come to the plate with the right kind of bat."

"Oh shit man, I don't want to jump through no rings, I just

want to be high." "I'm telling you, if you want more drugs you got to bring more money. If you want some of those better drugs, you got to bring even more money. Do you understand me? Am I being clear in your brain? And if you want more money you go to clean yourself up. You hearin' me boy?" "Yeah, I guess I hear you."

"I know a guy who can help you make more money if tha's what you want. This guy is a pro. He knows people. He got the connections. He makes things happen. He gets the job done. Yes, this man is a real professional." "What do I have to do?" Bob asked.

"I'll be seeing my friend later today. I'll tell him about you. Meet me here tomorrow."

Lerouy walked around the corner, pulled the cellular phone out of his hip pocket, then dialed. "Ronald, just take a look him. Hell you ain't goin' to have to break him in. He's been working the edges. You just need to dress him up a little. Maybe class him up a little. This boy could knock down some good money for you."

Bob had gone and worked Chart Street. He had done two guys, one in his car at the curb, and another stand-up in an alley. One of the two had only given him twenty bucks, the guy in the car. The asshole had ripped him off for twenty. Bob should have gotten the money before he did the gig. Sometimes he just spaced out. It was noon and already he was starting to come down, he'd have to go find Lerouy real soon. That forty he'd earned wasn't going to go very far. He could feel the sweat. Stomach cramps were just around the corner. Better leave the street and get to Lerouy quick. It wasn't a good day.

"It's all I got, man!" "Then this is all you're goin' to get. It's like I 'splayed to you yesterday, Roberto. I will sell you all the drugs you want, but you got to have the money. The money, son! This here is a cash and carry business."

"Man, there ain't enough here to keep me through two o'clock. I ain't gonna make it, Lerouy." "You goin' to make it, white boy. You goin' to drag your ass back out on the street and hustle up some more cash, if you want some more of this stuff, which you do!"

"Lerouy, I promise I'll have the money for you this afternoon, by five, just trust me man, give me a couple of peas."

"Trust a junky, shit. You got to be shittin' me man. And also, you hearing ain't none too good today, kind of like yesterday. I said this is a business, a cash and carry business. You dig? Fuck no, I ain't loanin' out no smack."

"Lerouy, I'll honest to God do anything you say. You want some sex? You can do anything you want to me! Just say it, I'll do it. Anything!"

"You fucked up junky, I wouldn't even fuck you with someone else's cock. I wouldn't fuck you if you were your sixteen-year-old sister. I ain't buyin' no sex, you dick head. I sell drugs for money. If I want to get laid, there is a lineup of fine lookin' females who will do it for free, just because they like my style. I sure as shit don't need a blowjob from some dirty, yellow-toothed junky. Shit, man!"

"I just need the smack, Lerouy."

"Okay, I'll tell you what you do. You call this number." Lerouy handed Bob a piece of paper torn out of a phone book with a phone number scribbled along the edge. "The man's name is Ronald. You tell Ronald that Lerouy asked you to call him." "Then what?"

"Then What? You do what the man says, you dipshit. Jesus, you ain't got the brains of a cockroach."

"I just wanted to know why I'm callin' him. That's all." "He's the man with the connections. He's the man who's goin' to get you into some money so's you can come and buy ol' Lerouy out of that really good shit, that pure white shit. You are goin' to be buyin' so much of that China white that ol' Lerouy is goin' to retire. Maybe buy a big yacht down toward Bimini Town. Hang some of that free pussy on it, and go fishin'. That's why you are callin' Mr. Ronald, so's ol' Lerouy can retire and go fishin'."

Bob booted the forty dollars worth of smack. He took his time enjoying the short high before calling Ronald. The phone connection was kind of in and out, like Ronald was talking while walking around or maybe driving. "Yes?"

"Ah, hello, Ronald?" "Who's this?" "Bob. I'm Bob. Lerouy said to call you. Is this Ronald?" "Yeah!" "Lerouy said to call you. He said to call you about making some money." "Yeah. What else Lerouy tell you?" "He said you got connections, and could help me make some good money." "What's he talking about, connections and money? Just what's all that about?" "Look man, Lerouy said you could help me make some good money. I don't know what it's all about. All I know is I gotta get some money today, before five." "Is that when you get sick?" "Yeah man! You know,

45

don't you?" "I know." "Then can you help me?" "Maybe." "Lerouy said to do whatever it was you wanted." "Oh, he said that? What else did he say?" "Ronald, Lerouy said to call you and do whatever you say cause you could help me make some good money. That's all I remember." "Okay boy, meet me two blocks north of where you usually meet Lerouy in half an hour." "Okay. Sure I'll do that. But I don't know what you look like." "I know what you look like. You just show up, hear?" "Sure!"

The dark maroon Brougham four door slowly cruised around the block twice, then parked at the curb several car lengths back from the intersection. Bob got there in time to see it make one pass. The windows were heavily tinted, so it was impossible to make out how many occupants were inside.

Bob waited at the intersection, unsure of what to do. He leaned against the lamppost hoping something would happen soon. A few cars came through the intersection. Some slowed for the intersection, and some, with tires chirping on the crosswalk paint, accelerated hard all the way through it. A couple of women walked past chatting to each other, both pulled little wire shopping baskets with wheels, but no cargo. Two men passed Bob walking in opposite directions and not acknowledging each other or Bob. Two minutes later, Bob saw the headlights flash on the Brougham.

"Get in the back seat," a very stern voice said, as the passenger side window glided down, and then up again. Bob got in at the right rear and closed the door. It locked behind him with a clunk. A very large mulatto man behind the steering wheel, half turned and looked at Bob from behind sunglasses. He then turned, started the car and slowly drove away from the curb. Carefully, the driver drove around several blocks, looking in the rearview mirrors for someone to be following. There was no one back there. The car was brought to the curb and the engine shut down. The driver again turned to look at Bob.

"Take your clothes off. Take off everything." "Look, I don't put out until after I'm paid," said Bob, fingering the top buttons of his shirt. The driver reached in his left front pants pocket, brought out a roll of bills, peeled off ten twenties and tossed them back into the back seat. Bob was stunned but recovered quickly, and began picking up the bills. "How do you want me to do it?" Bob asked, after stuffing the two hundred dollars into his left pocket. "Get your clothes off. Everything." "Sure," said Bob, quickly undoing his pants, then taking off his shoes, socks, shirt and underwear. "Ah, you are Ronald, right?" "Yeah, I'm Ronald all right. Now sit up so I can see you good." Bob sat straight on in the center of the big back seat, facing Ronald, and spread his legs wide enough so the man could get a look at his cock and balls. "This guy has paid enough for one hell of a good look, and anything else he wants," he thought to himself. "Lets see your arms." Ronald closely inspected both arms, slightly leaning over the back seat. "You about to really fuck up that left arm ain't you, boy? You got to start puttin' that needle where id don't show." Ronald continued his examination. "Let's see your dick." Bob lifted it with his left hand. "Pull the skin back and hold it so's I can see all around." "Now, turn around and bend over and spread your cheeks." Bob did it. "Except for being too skinny, at least outwardly you look okay. You got any diseases Bob?" "No man, I ain't got no diseases. Well, last week I had a little touch of the flu." "How much you usin'?" "I don't know, maybe a gram a day now." "You doin' anything other than smack?" "No. Just smack." "Okay. Now here is what I want you to do. You and I are takin' a little ride into town. I'm goin' to clean you up so's you can make some money. Not that nickel and dime shit you been into, but some real money son. You do want some of that real money, don't you?" "I want it." "All right then, away we go. Put your clothes back on. I am goin' to get you cleaned up. You look like a sack a shit." "Ronald, I need to see Lerouy before we go too far." "Here." Ronald tossed a small packet of white powder into Bob's direction. "Put that in your pocket for later." Bob immediately stuffed it into his left front pants pocket. This was his second gift. This was turning out to be a pretty good day. He wished he had his kit on him. It would be nice to jump on this fine looking smack right now.

Ronald parked the Brougham in front of a rundown looking hotel. In it's prime it probably housed traveling salesmen, on the way up and down, in this city's heart. The lobby was as worn as the exterior, with frayed carpet and drapes desperately in need of a thorough cleaning. Bob bobbed along after Ronald as they climbed to the second floor hallway, stopping midway down the hall where Ronald unlocked a door and led the way into a room.

The room was small with the barest of furnishings, a bed, and a nightstand with a small lamp on it, a small desk with two drawers on one side and a single upright chair. There was a window overlooking the brick wall of the building next door. On the ceiling was a fan with a single light bulb in the center. A tiny walk in closet, and a small bathroom, completed the quarters.

"This is your place now," Ronald said, "this is where you live, dig? This is where when I say go home, you come home to, get it?" Bob gave the room a quick look, then sat on the bed. The idea seemed bizarre. It was taking a while to sink in. Bob couldn't remember being here before. Sometimes things sort of went in and out of focus. "I live here now! Hey man, that's cool. I mean, this is really too cool."

"Now then Roberto, I want you to get out of those clothes, and get showered. There is plenty of soap, and towels to dry off with. You are to scrub your body until it's clean. When that has happened, and only after it has happened, you will get a new syringe, and kit. You may then want to get into that shit I gave you. Then we're going to clean that mouth of yours. I got a technician coming over here in a little while to take care of that little task. We are going to get you ready to make some money, boy!"

Bob felt the hot water flow over his body. It distracted him and for the moment eased his growing need for the heroin. He did as he was told and scrubbed using a bar of soap as a scrub brush. Ronald handed him a bottle of Head and Shoulders. He lathered his long hair. Bob's wiry unkempt beard collected shampoo and hot water running off the front of his face. It was the second time in two weeks he had showered. The water running to the drain this time was a lot less brown than before. Ronald however, was not altogether satisfied with the cleanliness and sent him through a second time with the bar of soap and a washcloth.

Ronald had taken all of Bob's clothes, pushed them into a paper bag and set the bag near the door for disposal. Laid out on the bed was a red long sleeved polo shirt with a little alligator on the left breast, a pair of tan khaki pants with a belt, underwear, and socks. "Get dressed in this stuff," Ronald said to Bob, when he had finished drying off.

Someone knocked at the door. Ronald opened it. A woman, in her late fifties, carrying a small makeup case walked into the room. Ronald closed the door behind her. "Enna, this is your project for the afternoon. His name is Bob. Where do you want him?"

Enna surveyed the room and said, "Probably have him lay on the bed near the edge where I can get at that mouth." Bob said, "Ain't I supposed to get some smack now? You said I'd get it now." "It's going to have to wait. We need you to work with Enna for a short while." "Man, I ain't feelin' too good," said Bob. "You just goin' to have to hang in there for a while. You'll be all right until Enna finishes your mouth, then you can put yourself on the nod," said Ronald. "Ronald, it's just that I ain't feelin' too good. I think I'm goin' to be sick." "Shit, Bob. All right, fix yourself up. But don't use those arms. Use your thighs or around your feet." Bob quickly prepared the heroin for injection with his new kit, which included a cigarette lighter to heat the white crystals and water in a large stainless steel serving spoon. He injected himself on the inside of his left thigh.

"Come over here and lay down on this side of the bed," Enna said, when Bob had finished the injection. "I'm going to put this towel around your front so's we don't soil that new clean shirt." Bob sat on the edge of the bed and swung his legs up, stretching out where Enna had pointed. "Bob, you're going to have to help me out. You're going to have to keep your mouth open for me. I don't want you going to sleep. Do you understand?" "Yes, I understand," said Bob, his pupils already beginning to constrict.

Enna opened her case and brought out a kidney shaped pan along with three dental cleaning tools, which she sat on the towel above Bob's stomach. "Okay, open up. Let's take a look," she said. "This is going to take a while," she shot a glance at Ronald. The cleaning took just under two hours, including eight trips to the sink in the bathroom to spit out the grunge Enna had scraped away. Bob had gone on the nod several times during the session. Fortunately Enna had started with the inside quadrants first so when Bob's mouth started involuntarily closing, she worked the lip side of the teeth. By the time she finished, his gums were bleeding enough to completely color his mouth red, making a bit of a mockery of the polish job she had so carefully done.

"Enna, that beard has got to go. What do you think?" "Hey Ronald, he's your boy. How do you want him?" "I think we goin' to try him clean faced." "Okay, I'll plug in my clippers. But first, open that window, I'm sweatin' like a horse!"

Ronald was amazed. When Enna had taken away all of the facial hair, the junky looked damned good. He had an attractive face, maybe a little feminine even. Enna had even brushed his long hair and tied it back to make a ponytail after trimming it and cutting away split ends. Bob cleaned up better than expected. He even looked a lot younger. Ronald guessed he was in his late twenties. "How old to you think he is Enna?" "Hummm, maybe twenty four, twenty five," she said. "He sure looks a damn site prettier than when I got here, doesn't he? "Just what I was thinkin'?" "When you putting him to work?"

Looking at his watch, Ronald said, "Probably in about two hours," with a smile. "I think I'd recommend that you wait for those gums to settle down first." "How long is that going to take?" "I think I'd wait until tomorrow sometime." "You know I got quite a little investment here. Already I'm out for a bag of China White, almost a grand. Two changes of clothes, there's another hun' and a half. If I didn't already own this hotel I'd be out for room rent. There's two hun' in cash I outright gave him, and then your services. And you ain't exactly cheap. I need to get him into action as soon as possible. We startin' out in the hole here! And bein' up this early is messin' up my sleep pattern.

"Ronald you know you'll put all this on his tab anyway, including room rent and the change of clothes. You are paying me to help keep him healthy and available, and I say he can go to work tomorrow, after the gums stop bleeding." "I guess I was gettin' in a hurry to test him out. Enna you really made him look good. I think he's goin' to be a big hit. When I get the chance I think we might see how he looks in makeup." "You putting him in drag?" "You know, with his build and face, he might look real good working that side, I get a lot of calls for that kind of action. And it pays better than the regular gay stuff. Yeah, I might use him as a TV."

"Well You aren't out a dime. I'm here now. He's here now. Let's throw a little makeup on him and see what we have. It might be interesting." "Okay, do it, while he's havin' this nice little nap." Enna brought out a selection of eye shadow, blush and lipstick, made a choice of each, and began applying them. It was unbelievable the change.

Bob's naturally feminine facial structure lent itself

perfectly to the coloring and shading. As Enna applied the lip-gloss, Bob brought his hand up to brush the stick away. "It's okay Bob, it's just me, Enna. Back to sleep you go." "Cool," Bob whispered, and smiled, and lay still. "What do you think, Ronald? Pretty snazzy, huh? Probably could use an eyebrow tweezing. But, how's she look?" "Jesus! I don't believe it! It just ain't the same person. It's a good lookin' woman I'm seeing here. Maybe not star quality, but lookin' good." "You just give me a chance to work on him a little bit, Ronald. I'll turn him into Meg Ryan for you." "Enna you definitely made a point here. I wouldn't have believed it if I hadn't seen it. He could pass for a she with the right clothes. Maybe even just the right under clothes. Maybe just a padded bra under a blouse, along with some girl's jeans would do it. No question about the effect. Jesus, you've uncovered a gold mine." "You lucked out with this one, Ronald." "Maybe I'll just put him on the street with that face on. No, no, I don't think so. This is too valuable for the street. This is out call material. Strictly big money out call!" Ronald's cellular phone rang. Business was beginning for the evening.

Gertrude looked up from her paperwork as Hansen strolled in past the glass doors of the office. "Have a nice day off?" "Better than nice, Gertrude thanks." "I've heard that any day in a Beechcraft is a great day." "You've heard correctly. And I trust you and Satchel were able to make us a lot of money while I was off?" "My turn to say that this time you are correct. We picked up a new account. See Satchel for the details. Two of our old clients talked to Satchel about some new business. Again see Mr. Green for details. And we received our last installment from Mr. Kogi, along with a note. Again, see Mr. G. for details on that note. The check has been deposited." "Anything else?"

"Let's see," she flashed her incredibly radiant smile, "yes, please sign these checks. Payroll and payables! And we're still solvent, not bad I'd say, for a little country firm in a big city."

"Has Satchel come in yet," he asked, picking up the small stack of checks. "He must still be here, he came in before me this morning." Hansen walked back to his office, and placed the papers he was carrying on his desk, then went in to Sachel's office. "We scored yesterday, I hear!" "Hey Bill. Yeah, we picked up a new client, Fiske Norge, and got some more work from Kiettl-Shotz, and Nebrur, S.A. And how was the day off?"

"It was mind clearing. I flew down to Nags Head again, and did my beach bum impression." "Bill, you've convinced me. I'm taking next Friday off. My daughter is sailing her El Toro in the club races. Francis and I want to spend the day tuning her up, and picnicking."

Hansen smiled, "What bunk, you got lucky, that's all. I don't see any craftsmanship in answering a phone, with people throwing money at you on the other end. I'll even bet they asked for me!" Green grinned, "Talk about cheeky! I slave over a hot phone line making this firm 'gazillions', and this is what I get?"

"I'll tell you what you get. You get to buy lunch. I mean literally, you are buying lunch. I don't have a dime on me," Hansen out grinned Green. "Did you come up from the beach just to mooch food?"

Hansen retained his grin and fluttered his eyebrows in affirmation. "Want to go NOW?" "It's only eleven, and you just got here." Hansen whispered, "Bring that note from Kogi, and let's get the hell out of here for a little bit." Green gave a nod of understanding. "Meet you at the front door in thirty seconds." "Gertrude, Satchel and I will be out of the office until two," Hansen was at the door. Satchel met him there.

"I'll be here. I'm not taking lunch today. My son and his new bride are taking me out for an early supper. I want to be good and hungry. It's payback time for him," she said. Both men nodded and went out the door.

"Kogi says we are officially off the payroll. Here's the note, read it. He says that the Kaji is planning on downgrading their expenditures for the U.S. operations; therefore they have chosen not to retain a full time agent in Washington. However, if the future dictates further needs, they will certainly consider past alliances when selecting someone to fill those needs."

Hansen reread the note a second time. It was simple and to the point. Terse, yet polite. He knew that Kogi was not overly verbal, but there was something in the note that said more than the words. They were out, that was certain, and because of the vote on 87788 Kogi felt they lacked the horsepower to make things happen. Hansen said, "You and I both know that not every lobbyist is successful all of the time. We did the best we were able. A couple of guys sold us out. How do you predict treachery? I don't have the answer."

"At least Kogi honored our contract with that last check," Green said, "Our cash flow stays intact. The business could actually not take anything in for a year, and we'd still be here with the doors open and the same staff. Thanks, of course to my splendid financial handling through the last couple of years. Not to pat myself on the back or anything!"

"Way to get us off this Kogi subject, Satch. And yes, you've done a masterful job of managing our income. I really do have to thank you for that. In fact I apologize for not saying something. Between you and Gertrude, our office couldn't be run better for any amount of money. Stanford taught you well."

"Stanford was a million years ago. I could go back and teach them a few things now. It certainly isn't all in the books. So, back to Kogi, What are your thoughts?"

"I guess as far as we're concerned Kogi and his Kaji are history. I wouldn't expect any more business from them. Knowing Kogi as I do, I believe this thing hasn't gone away. He is undoubtedly still in pursuit of 87788. It's so dangerous to them, that even if it becomes law, they'll go on fighting it even if it takes ten years. The consequences are enormous, but then we already knew that going in. Consequently, the funding from Tokyo is also enormous. And the demand to get quick results justifies the cubic dollar expenditure they have made, to blow 87788 away. I wouldn't be surprised if Kogi was behind the neat little scenarios we've seen on TV lately. He certainly has access, which he learned about from us. And I wouldn't be at all surprised if a lot more heavy stuff came down on this one. In that respect, I think we're off the hook. Kogi probably just sees us as incompetent, not as antagonists."

"So is this the limit of our conversation on the subject? If so, why didn't we have it back in the office, Bill?"

"Satch, I don't know what Kogi has planned, but my intuition tells me it's going to be tough. Someone is going to get leaned on pretty heavy. I think individual safety may be at great risk here."

"Do you mean our safety, yours and mine? Lay this idea out, Bill. Or, if it's not us at risk, then who?"

"Maybe Phillbroom, maybe Hillby, maybe Cask. Those names standout as the heaviest at risk, in my little scenario. In my opinion, the Kaji, through Kogi are very capable of sanctioning almost anyone. I don't know if Phillbroom, Hillby, or Cask has any notion about the jeopardy of opposing Kogi. But I remember my first reaction to the passage of 87788 in the Senate, that someone is going to get hurt big time. There is nothing that we can point to and say that there has been a threat, or that anyone was threatened at anytime, for that matter. That's a problem. If the threat existed, then we could get security involved. As it is, I just can't roll up to Phillbroom and say that someone may take a pot shot at him or something, especially if I had to name Kogi as the suspect. When word got around, and word would get around, that I accused Kogi of a plot to harm Phillbroom, Kogi would come down on me like a ton of bricks. In fact it might just be a ton of bricks. Satch, I feel that we need to do something, but I don't know what it would be at this point."

"My God, I see why you didn't want to talk about this in the office. Although I trust Gertrude and the two office girls, I agree that this sort of thing could get out of hand real quick if someone, however innocently, started talking about it outside the office. You're right, it would all come back to us. We could get our butts kicked. I also agree that the possibility of real violence in this situation exists. And, I don't have any clue at all as to how we should approach our dilemma. I don't think we're ready for the FBI or John Wayne."

"All we can do is keep our eyes and ears open, I guess. Any little thing that gets stirred up to the surface should be analyzed and discussed by the two of us. If indeed something overt happens, then we give it to the law."

Hamilton met each of his chosen five at his front door with the usual robust handshake, and a bear hug. His pleasure at seeing each of them was quite apparent. Their reaction to him was the same. It was the first time they had all been together since leaving for their respective target city. There was a great feeling of comradeship that pervades any group that has obtained its difficult goal. Because of the clandestine nature of their operation, there was no one and no place other than here where their sense of fulfillment could be adequately and openly expressed.

"My land, it's sure fine seeing all of you again. I do appreciate the difficulties you have been through since the last time we were here in this room together. You have had to sacrifice your personal lives, exercise deceit with loved ones as well as strangers. Live in places that you would not be inclined to think about twice as your choice of living areas. You have had to deal with some of the lowest of human elements. You have had to perform tasks that were, well, let us say distasteful to you. You have, no doubt, gone against your very nature. However, you have prevailed. You have born your tasks like true soldiers, like Christian soldiers.

You have carried out a guerrilla operation whose impact will change mankind in a most positive way, by ridding it of perverted elements. Elements whose morality has been thrown in the face of every Christian in this country of ours for the past thirty years. We Christians are now fighting back, thanks to what you've all done, and through a disease that has God's design written onto it for cleansing the world.

Now the most difficult part of the operation begins. It is imperative that everyone in this room maintains silence about what has been done. Can I safely assume that you have collectively told no one of our program?"

There were murmurings of "No one" and heads shaking. "The safety of everyone resides with each person here. A breach of security by any one person will have consequences for all.

You must individually forget about your activities after this meeting. For the moment however, let's salute ourselves for a job well done." Silver trays filled with oysters on the half shell, freshly opened, were set on the table in front of everyone. With shots of Tabasco, and squeezes of lemon, the trays were emptied quickly. Hamilton, who said he was refraining because of his gout, poured out the contents of a bottle of cold, sparkling apple juice into champagne glasses, then passed the tray of glasses around. When each person had one, he raised his glass in salute. "Godspeed, everyone!" "Godspeed," came their reply. Hamilton raised his glass to his lips. The chosen five followed suit and drained theirs.

The first to react to the toxin was a very thin man in his late sixties. Shortly, the other four, followed the first and onto their knees, then down to the floor grasping at their throats. Death for all five came within minutes. Hamilton calmly walked to the phone and dialed 911.

The evening news broadcasts all carried the tragic story of the death of five prominent people due to shellfish poisoning. The deaths occurred at a party given by Felton Hamilton in his lavish home. Mister Hamilton, when reached by phone, said he was in shocked disbelief at manner of loss of his closest friends, and was deeply, deeply saddened, and shaken.

Chapter 10

"Ridin' High"

Pieces of broken concrete were thrown at the large plate glass windows until three were broken out. The missiles, along with large and small fragments of glass, dug chips of paint off the new Cadillacs on the showroom floor. A twenty-year-old convertible on center display in the showroom, received a broken windshield, cuts in the leather seats, and dents on the right front door and fender from the attack. Its carefully preserved original condition was forever altered.

Two tall men in ski masks jumped onto the outside windowsill and spray painted the remaining window with "Big Business Collusion", "Kill That Bill". They then leaped back to the ground and lost themselves in the angry crowd.

Rendel Schultz screamed through the bullhorn, "Kill that

bill!" The crowd, numbering well over one hundred voices, loudly took up the chant, "Kill that bill!" Fists pummeled the air, and signs, with the same words, were thrust above the grim shouting faces. Three TV cameras recorded Pulitzer Prize winning shots over the running commentary of Glen Glege.

"My God, did you see that. They destroyed the showroom right in front of us! I can't believe this is happening. But now, I can, yes; I can hear the sirens heading this way. The police are seconds away. There is the first patrol car turning the corner a block away and coming fast down Telegraph. It looks like a canine patrol car. The officer has stopped the car a short distance away from the North end of the crowd, and is talking into his microphone. I hear more sirens. Here come, it looks like perhaps, a dozen or more patrol cars. And yes, there are a couple of CHP cars." Glege was now shouting over chants of, "Sold us out, sold us out."

Men in business suits stood in the Service drive breezeway of the dealership, staring out at the mob. They were flanked by a few mechanics armed with heavy hand tools. A couple of the mechanics were making gestures that in body language said, "let's get 'em!" One of the men in a business suit turned toward the mechanics shaking his head, and speaking to them with his back to the mob. The cameramen got it all.

Rendel Schultz put the bullhorn to his mouth at the same moment an automobile fuel pump, thrown by a mechanic and aimed at the same spot, arrived. The bullhorn deflected the fuel pump that cracked the plastic case and broke the electronic amplifying mechanism in the bullhorn. The impact cut Schultz's lower lip that bloodied his mouth and beard. A full-scale fight instantly followed the impact, as seven mechanics dived into the center of the crowd surrounding Schultz.

Fists were flying. People tried to push away from the brawl but were held in place by those in the rear straining to get a better look at what was going on. Twenty people from the crowd went down as fighters fell into them or tripped over them. A cameraman went down breaking the video camera as he and four others fell on it. It's signal stopped. A dozen helmeted, uniformed policemen forced their way into the storms eye and began separating those throwing blows. Bloodied noses, lips, and knuckles prevailed. Some of those on the ground held a hand to an eye or rubbed an ankle, groaning. The separated fighters continued to shout insults across the short blue line of policemen as another dozen-riot protection clad policemen pushed their way into the now docile crowd.

Rendel Schultz was pulled to his feet. His face was bloody from the split lip, and from several blows landed by one of the mechanics. With his face a foot away from one of the mechanics who was being held back by a policeman, he yelled, "You cocksucker, I'm going to come back here and stomp the shit out of you." With that, the policeman temporarily lost control of the mechanic who landed a solid right fist in Schultz's belly. "Fuck you. Go get a job, asshole," the mechanic yelled back, as two additional riot police shoved him back. Schultz went to the ground with the wind knocked out of him.

Another two-dozen police were on the scene within ten minutes. It was clear that the altercation was over as those who were unscathed helped those who were downed to hobble away down the street in both directions. Those who looked as if they were directly involved in the fight were detained, separated into two groups and eventually taken away in police vans. Schultz went in the first van. Spectators, and some of the remaining mob were told to move along. They disbursed at their own rates.

Glen Glege and the TV crew remained with cameras running. Glege interviewed some of the staff at the dealership. No one knew what stimulated the attack on the showroom. "We were sitting there working. Then we heard glass breaking," said the business manager. "Those idiots should be locked up, they could have really hurt someone," she said. One of the others in the business office said she was glad that some of the men in the service department had stopped the attack. It was clear that she was worried about her personal safety. Glege directed the cameras to zoom in on the writing on the remaining showroom window. "Big Business Collusion". "Kill That Bill." "And now back to you at the station. This is Glen Glege signing off from Berkeley."

Kogi was pleased. He loved to see Americans fighting in the street. When the scenes were viewed in Tokyo it brought more credulity to his demands for a greater budget for security. "Americans are a violent group of people, this is what we must face every day here in the States. If I am to protect my people, my workers, then you must pass this increased budget plan, immediately." It worked. The plan was passed and funded the same afternoon. In reality, Kogi now had enough money for a lot more head bashing and broken windows on the TV news. After all the talent for these scenes was cheap. Schultz, the most expensive of the group, was only a hundred a day. Rent-a-mob was cheaper today than a few years ago. It made sense, these were hard times.

Phillbroom's aid, Charles, moved his head closer in order to hear the Senators whispered words. The aid, a tall, well proportioned man about thirty, arose from the table, walked to where their waiter was standing, and inquired as to the whereabouts of a telephone. The young man headed to where the waiter had suggested, with the eyes of several females in the room following him.

Phillbroom loved the food but hated the restaurant for invoking a no smoking rule. He'd have sold his soul for one of his Cuban's right now.

When she walked past, he lost all thoughts of cigars. His mind clicked back to nineteen forty-five. This good looking twenty year old had run up to him as they were marching, kissed him on the lips, welcomed him back to the U.S.A, passed him her phone number on a slip of paper, then walked back into the crowd that stood watching the parade. He watched her walk. Her beautiful female walk. Yes, she was definitely what they had been fighting for. He had called twice. She wasn't home. They had never connected, but he never forgot that walk. And now that walk had just gone past his table. He turned and followed her with his eyes as she, and a young man and woman, took a table across the room. The face was faint, but the memory was strong.

Charles came back to the table. "We'll have the tickets by courier in the morning," Charles said sitting down.

"That's excellent. You know, the more I think about it, the

better this little vacation idea sounds." Phillbroom was ecstatic. "A little ol' Southern fishin' trip, tied to a couple days of good food in New Orleans. A little roughin' it, smoothed over by the French Quarter. It was a genius of an idea. With any kind of luck, it could smooth out a few wrinkles, isn't that right Charles?" Phillbroom grinned.

Charles answered with a smile, "I expect we may be some of the luckiest people, Senator." "I'll just hold you to that," Phillbroom smiled, and winked.

Phillbroom's gaze returned momentarily to the lady with the walk at the far table. Charles noticed immediately and said, "She certainly is an attractive woman."

"Yes, she's a very handsome woman, especially for her age." Phillbroom tried to downplay his acute attraction to her. "And she reminds me of someone from a long time ago."

"Someone you knew well Senator?" Charles asked with a knowing smile. "No, someone I'd have liked to have known well, Charles." Phillbroom motioned the waiter over. "Can you find me something to write on?" "Why of course Senator, how much paper do you need?" "How about a page from that little order pad you carry, George." "Certainly sir." George handed him two pages of three by five blank paper. Phillbroom took the pen offered by Charles and scrawled a few words. "George." "Yes Senator?"

"Please take this to the lady at the far table, there to my right. The one who is sitting with the young man and woman." "The lady in the dark blue suit?" "Yes that one.

Oh and take a good bottle of champagne with that note."

"I'll see to it sir." George walked to the wine steward, said a few words, then went to the kitchen. In less than a minute George emerged from the kitchen with the waiter at who's table the lady was seated. That waiter carried a small silver tray with the Senators note, and was followed by George bearing a bottle of champagne. A white-coated young man carrying a standing wine cooler waited unobtrusively near the kitchen door to be summoned.

"Excuse me mademoiselle, this is from the tall mature gentleman seated four tables over," the waiter extended the silver tray. The lady took the note. "And he has sent this as well," he motioned; George stepped up beside him presenting the bottle, not speaking.

"Mother!" the young man squealed, and smiled at her. "What is going on?" The lady reread the note twice, then gently smiled, and slowly looked up from the note. The young man and woman looked at each other questioningly, and shrugged their shoulders.

"May we serve the wine mademoiselle?" the waiter asked. Gertrude smiled, thought for a moment, and said," Yes, that will be fine." The waiter summoned the wine cooler. George opened the bottle and handed it to the other waiter who poured.

Gertrude touched her son's arm and said, "Please excuse me for just a moment. This is from Senator Phillbroom. I must go over and thank him."

She got up from the table, note in hand, with her waiter

sliding the chair back, and walked to the Senator's table. Her walk was slightly exaggerated, and self-conscious. Phillbroom could not take his eyes off of her. She had that certain something that for lack of better words is called an incredibly strong personal attraction. It forced him, beyond good manners, to explore her body and especially that wonderful walk, with his eyes and his complete consciousness as she came toward him. Gertrude was innately aware of it.

"Senator Phillbroom," she said as the Senator rose from his chair, "I am completely flabbergasted by your recall." She extended her hand.

Phillbroom took her hand in both of his. "My dear lady, I do hope you'll forgive my boldness, sending that note. I knew it was you, and I just had to solve one of the long time mysteries in my life."

"Senator, I really don't know how you can remember one teenaged girl from so long ago." "You left quite an impression on me. But you know something, I don't even know your name." She blushed slightly. "So a telephone number was all I gave you?"

"Well, that and a lasting impression."

"I'm Gertrude. In those days, I was Gertrude Sonderquist. When I married I became Gertrude Steen. My husband died about ten years ago, but I kept his name."

"Gertrude. Gertrude Steen," he repeated. "It is truly wonderful to see you again after all those years. I can see that those years have rested mighty fine on you. You're as trim as a schoolgirl."

"Thank you Senator, you're very kind," she said in an amused way, thinking that his demeanor represented the last of Southern chivalry.

"Please, Gertrude, call me Harry."

"Okay Harry!"

"You know, I don't know where my manners went. Gertrude, this young man is Charles, my most valued new assistant." They offered their hands and hellos.

"Harry, thank you for the champagne."

"You are indeed welcome. Perhaps you'd be kind enough to indulge me on another occasion and join me for dinner?"

"I would like that very much Harry."

"We unfortunately have this evening spoken for, but may I call you Gertrude?"

"Certainly, I'll write my home phone on the back of my card." She smiled and took a business card from the pocket of her jacket and wrote the number on it.

Phillbroom handed her his card. She thought, God I already have these numbers on my desk in the Rolodex. She exchanged cards and said, "Thanks. And I suppose I should get back to my little party."

"Of course Gertrude. Thank you for acknowledging my

note, and coming over. Charles and I have to run as well. We have a committee meeting that we may just be on time for." He took her hand, shook it gently. "May I call you later in the week?"

"Of course."

"Well then, I'll wish you a very pleasant evening, Gertrude."

"Pleasant evening, Harry. Nice meeting you Charles."

"My pleasure, Gertrude, good night," Charles smiled.

Gertrude walked back to her table, as the two men left. Her son, a bemused look on his face said, "Mother. Care to explain?"

She opened the note and handed it to him. He read it out loud to his wife. "V.E. Day parade, New York City 1945. You kissed me then disappeared. I called, you weren't home." He looked at his mother in a new perspective. "When did you meet him, Mom?"

"Tonight is the first time, formally. You had to have been there when the war ended, at least the war in Europe ended. People were high on being alive, the war ending, all those men coming home. I guess you really just had to be there to appreciate where we all were with it. I saw this good-looking guy in his uniform in the parade, who stood out because he was taller than most of those around him. I was young. I just ran up to him and kissed him, and left him my phone number."

"You really are a romantic Mom," the young man smiled at his new wife, squeezing her hand under the table.

"Anyone want to join me in a glass of bubbly," she asked? "To romance," she toasted. The champagne was first class.

Hamilton closed his business for a week of mourning for the five friends. Naturally, he continued his employee's compensation as usual. The church elders sent letters of condolences to him as well as to the families of those who had died so tragically. Hamilton made it clear that he felt responsible for those deaths, and would participate, along with the insurance companies, in providing benefits to those left behind. The newspapers praised his generosity. Only two of the five bereaved families accepted Hamilton's check. The others sent their checks back saying he was under no obligation, and they knew his anguish was nearly as great as theirs. "Go in peace," they had written on the thank you cards.

Funeral services for the five were worked out in order to give each group access to the other's services, as many of the mourners were common to all five-funeral parties. Hamilton rode as honored guest with each of the five families. His shoulders sagged, and there was grayness in his face.

A fresh bottle of J and B scotch sat on the top of the folding bar with about a forth of it gone. Two empty Schweppes Club Soda bottles were laying along side it. Hamilton felt comfortable in his office. He was the only one in the building. The scotch tasted clean. Soldiering had given him an appreciation of a victory drink at the appropriate time. Now was that time. The tension in his body began to melt away, telling him that the whiskey was working, and to be careful that he didn't overindulge. The world outside knew him as an extremely responsible person. That image, especially now must be maintained. There would be no thought of leaving the building until the liquor wore off. His car could be seen parked in its usual parking place in front of the building. He spent so much time at the business, that the appearances would be normal. A few hours ago the last of the dear Christian soldiers had been laid to rest. People would understand that he might immerse himself in his work at a time like this.

The soldiers would have understood. They died for the greater good. The plan had to survive. There would be no chance for leakage now. The idea had come to him almost at the last minute. The difficulty had been, getting the toxin. It had been obtained at a price, as usual, and with no questions asked. The later came built in to the price.

Bob's first week "on the job" produced some fine results. Carefully dispensed as an out call to gay men, he made, according to Ronald, nearly five hundred dollars above expenses. Naturally, the expenses included the heroin he consumed as provided by Ronald, the room, and a management fee. Ronald took him and was there to pick him up after the gig. He had only worked three nights, two gigs per night.

Ronald had not insisted that Bob wear female clothing; only that Enna cut and styled his hair in a more feminine fashion. When Enna came to do his hair, she brought a couple of shopping bags with girl clothes, from underwear to a suit. It also included black stockings and a garter belt to hold them up.

Bob made no pretenses; he was in it for the drugs. The money didn't mean much. Ronald supplied the drugs, and made it perfectly clear that he was the only one from then on who would indeed provide Bob with drugs. It was all part of the verbal management agreement that existed between the two of them, Ronald explained nicely. Lerouy, who also supplied Ronald, was told to not sell anything to Bob. Lerouy understood perfectly. He would still be providing the drugs to Bob, only through Ronald. It worked for him. The amount and quality were up which made him more money. The purchases were steadier too.

Bob went along with every turn of Ronald's program. When he was on a job, he was pleasant, cooperative, and docile, didn't expend a lot of energy, and didn't hang around when the gig was over. He handed over all the money to Ronald without trying to skim. His only drawbacks were his flat personality and his drug infatuation, and maybe he was a little too quiet for some of the clients. He had learned to give good head before he met Ronald, and he wasn't upset when he had to allow penetration. There was never any discussion about using condoms. If the customer wanted to use them it was, of course okay with him. Without was okay as well. Nearly all used a lubricant.

Ronald, through Enna, monitored Bob's health. She carefully inspected him weekly. Any problem was treated promptly and properly. Personal hygiene was lectured, and administered if found lacking. Enna had him taking six grams of vitamin C a day along with a one-a-day vitamin and mineral tablet. Ronald made sure he had at least one meal a day at the cafe, next door to the hotel. Ronald owned the cafe. As a result of the improved lifestyle, Bob's health improved radically over his days on the street.

Ronald's cellular phone rang. "Hi Steve. Yes I can take care of you. How many of you are there? Okay! You want a guy or a girl? If that is what you want, sure, I have that available. But it's a bit more expensive. Okay, but it's going to be fifteen hundred, cash. Okay, what time? He'll see you then." He broke the connection and redialed.

The hotel had plenty of parking spaces. The Brougham was parked at the entrance. Ronald went up to the second floor, and knocked on the door. He then let himself in with a key. Bob was just waking. "Okay Roberto, it's show time." Ronald walked to the closet, opened the door, and began shuffling through the clothes. A key slid into the door lock, the door opened, and Enna came into the room.

"Hey Enna, thanks for coming over on a short notice. We need to get our friend here put together for a special gig tonight."

"Special huh, just how special," Enna asked?

"Tonight Roberta is going to strut some stuff. It's her coming out party!"

"Well, all right!" "Yes sir." "Then we better do things right. Bob, get out of that bed and get into the shower, and shave, while I get some makeup out of this case and find the right clothes."

Bob did as he was told with a taciturn "Okay."

Enna opened up the bottom desk drawer, took out a

package of black nylon stockings, a black lace garter belt, black lace panties, and a padded black lace brassiere. She laid them on the bed, pushed Ronald aside, and pulled a short black velvet long sleeved dress from a hanger in the closet. "Now we're gettin' somewhere," she said. "Whoa, can't forget shoes and handbag," as she kneeled down and brought up some black short heeled pumps and a small black handbag.

"That must have set me back a few bucks," Ronald said, as he felt the material in the dress.

"You know it did," Enna answered. "Good stuff always shows good too."

Enna did an extraordinary make up job. It took nearly an hour, including the touch up on the hairdo. Roberta looked fantastic. As the underclothing went on, the transformation became astonishing.

"Okay Bob, put the shoes on and let's see a trial run. Just walk around the room, honey."

"Jesus Enna, you did a fantastic job," Ronald said, "I have a hard time remembering there is a guy under that stuff. He is going to be an absolute hit at tonight's ball, he, he!"

"Yeah, I got that," Enna said without smiling. "That is what this business is all about, now isn't it?"

"This one is going to be a winner for sure." Then, to Bob he said, "When was the last time you got high?"

"Just before I fell asleep. I don't know, maybe couple of

hours ago. I was just thinkin' I could use a hit. I'm sure not going to make it through tonight without it!"

"We got nearly two hours before you have to be downtown, so here, go ahead and use this." Ronald held out a very small packet of China white. But do the stuff right now. We got to finish gettin' you ready. I need to shave those legs. But first of all, let's see you walk in those shoes."

Bob had no trouble walking in the kitten-heeled shoes. Enna showed him how to place his feet in order to make the walk more feminine. The hip movement wasn't quite right, but that would take more time than they had at the moment. Enna felt that the look would be enough to get the point across on tonight's job. They could work on the walk another time.

As Bob went into the bathroom to shoot up, Ronald's cellular phone rang. Ronald answered," Yes? Yes, Clara is available. Okay give me your name, phone number, and address. When would you like her there? Okay, I'll call you back within ten minutes."

Ronald hung up, and redialed. "Jessie, I have a Clara outcall at nine, downtown Ramada. Can you make it? All right, girl." He gave her the name, address and phone number. "I'll call him back. Check in with me after? And don't forget, you have that couple at the Holiday Inn at eleven. Better take a cab, I'm going to be tied up. By for now." He hung up and dialed again. "Roland Clarke's room please. Mr. Clarke, Clara will call you just before nine. Yes, that's correct. Good by."

Ronald hung up. "Well, everyone is working tonight. That

Jessie now has two gigs. Marion is booked 'til two A.M.. Rosie is working at a party in the suburbs. Jolene has another party with the usual politicos. And Henry is suckin' some dicks of some payin' customers in Chinatown. That's what I call a good night."

Enna brushed the short black dress. "We all gonna be millionaires real soon," she smiled at Ronald.

"Can't be soon enough for me," he said, making notes in his little notebook.

Phillbroom pounded on the table with both fists. "Hot damn boys! Well done. Well done. You got the son of a bitch." The five men laughed and applauded themselves. Clive Cording's House Bill had been drilled full of holes in Committee, it wouldn't get out of the House. Cording had made some enemies by a negative vote on a tax bill four months earlier. He had made the two other Representatives from his home state, who had voted yes, look real bad back home. They had all originally agreed to a yes vote. In voting no, he was a hero of the people. Voting yes, they were the money-grabbing politicians. Phillbroom's staff with reminders of Cording's ballot treachery heavily prospected these same enemies. They turned his Bill to toast.

Phillbroom's staff, who had fumbled the ball initially, had come back with the simple plan under the tutorage of Charles, Phillbroom's new assistant. Charles had, at times, uncanny political savvy. His intervention with the staff in this Cording thing had saved all their jobs. It was evident that it may also have saved the Senator's Bill, 87788. Both the Senator and the staff were aware of each circumstance.

If there were Charles stock available, it would have jumped twenty-five points and have been bought out before this staff meeting ended. He had only been aboard for twelve days. Already Phillbroom was thinking about the possibility of grooming the boy to take over for him when he retired in a few years. Yes, the boy had it all, tall masculine good looks, intelligence, competence, a fine understanding of politics and timing, and he was a workaholic. He could go far if he wished it.

When the idea for a mini-vacation came along (it was Charles' idea) the Senator had initially thought to take Charles along to handle whatever little matters that might come up, so he could concentrate on relaxing. Now, after Cording was torpedoed, Phillbroom was thinking about spending some time feeling him out for his political aspirations as well. Perhaps it was a little premature, but the young man did show real promise. And he obviously had his ear to the political ground. Charles could be the son he never had. Now that statement really was premature. Those thoughts passed through Phillbroom's mind as the meeting closed.

Charles acknowledged the pats on the back from the staff with a smile, and not a lot of surface emotion, almost a business as usual posture, nearly what might be described as nonchalance. He stood up and shuffled some papers into his hand tooled leather brief case, and said "See you in the morning," in answer to their "Good Night."

"Well, I really do want to thank you again for your leadership. Those boys were pretty upside down before you jumped in," the Senator said after the last of the staff had left the room.

"I guess I was able to help a bit. Sometimes a fresh approach helps a situation."

"I don't think it was a fresh approach that did it, more like really knowing what the hell to do, and having an insight on a issue. That is what saved everyone's bacon this time. You're a little too modest this time Charles."

"Senator," Charles smiled wryly, "it's amazing sometimes how much information gets chucked on the table, in the form of gossip, at a friendly Tuesday night poker game. For some reason, stuff like that, I retain. Might be a family curse."

"Those are some powerful fine genes, young man. Wish I had them myself."

"Oh, but you do, Harry. That's what makes you such a good politician. You know and recall happenings around you better than nine-tenths of everyone in this entire government. There are a lot of terribly bright people here in Washington, but not enough who have the horse sense that you have to go with it."

"I do believe I could listen to you talk about me all night, son. And, I think you just did a pretty fine job of taking the spotlight off yourself and putting it on me. So, let me thank you this time for the spotlight as well as your effort on this Cording affair."

"You are welcome on both counts, Senator."

Bill Hansen, and Satchel Green had been in Hansen's office all morning, with the door closed. The nearly soundproof walls had rocked many times from their loud voices. They had blocked out two phone lines for their use, and one of those line indicator lights had been on almost constantly the entire morning. At eleven forty-five, Hansen came out, his shirtsleeves rolled up and his face flushed beyond his tan. "Gertrude, will you send one of the kids out for sandwiches and coffee?"

"No coffee, make mine a mineral water," came Satchel's voice.

"Make that one coffee and one mineral water, American mineral water please," Hansen emphasized the last phrase. "Mister health nut in there will have his usual vegetarian sandwich on seven grain bread, and I'll have roast red pepper and provolone on Italian, grilled."

Gertrude had begun writing at his first words. "Gotcha! I'll call the order in. Anything else?"

"Have you eaten yet Gertrude?"

"No?"

"Well, order something for yourself, and the kids as well, if they're hungry."

"Right," she said, and wrote another three sandwiches onto the order. "Girls, boss H is buying sandwiches. I'll have Fava's deliver."

Hansen walked back into the office and closed the door. "Now Satchel, before you say anything else, let me say this about Cording. He is a jerk. No, he's a first class jerk."

"Aren't you being a little too kind here?"

" The fact that he thinks we blew the whistle on him with his colleagues, and won't listen to us being innocent, bothers the hell out of me too."

"It bothers me," Satchel began, "that we may have such a reputation that people look to us when they see kinky things happening. It doesn't make any sense that we would want to spoil his Bill. Cording's accusation isn't logical. He should look to Phillbroom or one of Phillbroom's associates as the assassin. Now, that makes sense. Instead, he grinds on us for the better part of a morning. He was so far off base. I've talked to some unreasonable people in my life, but that two hour phone call was the craziest I've ever been witness to."

"It's history, Satch. He was obviously blowing off steam. He blew himself out. We didn't do it. Sooner or later he'll realize that. I vote we chalk this up to a blown morning."

"A blown morning," Satchel grinned, "rest in peace!"

"To change the subject, what say we start earning some money? Let's get hold of those fish consumption figures for Norge Fiske. If you'll do it, I'll begin writing the import proposal."

"Done deal, I prefer working the statistics."

"I knew that."

"In Berkeley," Glege said, reading the prompter, "overnight two auto dealerships have been hit by vandals. Monk Ford on San Pablo Avenue, and Bengt Chrysler on University, suffered broken windows and damage to new cars on display."

The monitor screen showed scenes of broken large windows, and showroom cars with "Big Business Collusion, and "Kill that Bill," spray-painted on their sides and hoods.

"Police responded to two different alarms at two A.M., but those involved had fled. Sergeant Rominowsky, spokesman for the Berkeley Police said, in an interview a few minutes ago, that both break-ins were under investigation. Apparently, nothing was taken, but repair costs to buildings and vehicles are expected to run into the thousands of dollars. Sergeant Rominowsky said that the vandalism in these two dealerships were similar to the one at the Cadillac Dealership ten days ago. That particular incident happened, however, in daylight, and involved a large group protesting a Senate Bill restricting imports. At the moment it is not known if this was the same group that struck again twice last night."

On camera, a sheet of paper was passed to Glege. "This just in, a caller, who identified himself as Rendel Schultz, spokesman for the Coalition For Lower Living Costs, has informed our news director that his group is responsible for the damage to both car dealerships. He says, and I quote, 'this action will continue, until Senate Bill 87788 is killed. The workingman is fed up with higher costs of living. And supporting Big Business gobbles up the little company he works for, then puts him out of work.' Schultz said he was still suffering from a broken finger that occurred outside the Cadillac dealership when thugs, hired by the dealership, tried to break up their demonstration. The caller didn't elaborate further."

"After these messages, we'll return for a story from the Oakland Zoo." On the monitor appeared a picture of an elephant throwing dirt in the air, which faded into the first commercial.

Kogi was, again, pleased with the way it was handled. The timing was perfect with the phone call. The station had shown the slogans. That was important. The way the reports came to the public was different and refreshing. It made an impression. It also made good copy in Japanese newspapers as well as those in the U.S. Kogi knew that those back home would be more pleased with themselves at having provided the extra funding for Kogi's corporate security, after reading about this latest hooliganism.

The only negative was Rendel Schultz who, after the broken finger incident, was asking for more money. Kogi's answer, through the usual intermediary, was to offer a sizable bonus if Schultz would see the project through to the end. The costs associated with the finger repair were already handled by the group's medical insurance. In the end, the bonus was agreed to. Kogi wondered if Schultz would ultimately collect it.

Kogi's apparent setback on Cording's Bill was used as cover for Charles. A new designate would be found shortly. And a new House answer to Phillbroom's Bill would again rise out of the Cording ashes. The language would be a variant of one it preceded but the result, if voted into law, would be the same. Sight of the goal was never lost.

The shrimp gumbo was so hot it burned his lips, tongue, and the roof of his mouth. Hamilton quickly dropped the spoon and took a long draw on the scotch and soda. It was the first food he'd had all day. He was as hungry as a panther. The whisky had accelerated that hunger. Now the food was in front of him, and he couldn't eat it. It made him angry. "How in the world did they ever get it so hot," he said aloud. "It must have taken them at least ten minutes to deliver it here. Should have cooled enough to eat by now." The tenderness in his mouth remained, along with the splendid flavor of the gumbo. Now he knew he'd have to wait until it completely cooled, in deference to the injured mouth, to eat it. He consumed the drink and quickly made another, adding more ice. The alcohol was making him careless and he knew it, maybe losing it a little. After all, he knew better than to stuff a whole spoon of soup into his mouth without testing it first. He made the decision to stay overnight in the office. It was a good decision. The scotch bottle was empty.

Phillbroom was in process of clearing his desk in the Senate chambers. Debate on a Wet Lands Bill had been hot and heavy. Printed material from Sierra Club lobbyists had obliterated his desktop. Some of the more militant Club members had sent faxes that threatened a recall movement if he didn't vote the proper way. This stack of faxes was placed in a green folder, and kept separate from other constituent correspondence on the subject. All of the paper, he collected and placed in specific order in his briefcase. The debate would resume in two days, after a recess.

He had once been an avid duck hunter, now he only had the opportunity to hunt a day or two each year. Like most hunters, he admired the animal he sought. Increasing breeding grounds encouraged reproduction and the subsequent increase in numbers available to be harvested. He therefore personally favored legislation that would increase habitat. Unfortunately there would ultimately be the Senators who were heavily driven by real estate interests to be overcome. The real estate interests were backed up by the League of City and County Governments, who were, of course, interested in extending tax bases, and were involved in political clout back home. A fine line had to be walked if the Bill ever got passed by the Senate. There was, however, no question as to how Phillbroom would vote.

Walking back to his office, Phillbroom thought about his earlier days as a hunter. The wonderful roast duck, the smoked duck salad, the duck sausages, the duck gumbo, pictures of richly set tables and of campfire suppers filled his head. "A well spent youth," he thought. His youth. The war. The Army. Coming home from Germany, and the girl from the parade. The picture warmed him again. He would call Gertrude this evening.

His wife had passed away seven years ago. Even though his life was filled with work, social engagements, and even travel, there was a void in the fullness of it. An occasional woman who, by political design or her own agenda, wound up in his bed overnight. But it wasn't the same as having someone, totally of his own choosing to share his life with. After all, he wasn't twenty, or thirty anymore, in fact he almost wasn't sixty anymore. Sex wasn't as important as it use to be. Time flew past. Maybe it was time again to find someone to spend the remainder of his life with. The walk in the warm afternoon sun had spun him into these thoughts of his personal life. It was a welcome break from the concentrated thinking of law making, and it changed his view of the afternoon. There was grass, a blue sky with very high horse tail clouds, and trees with birds chattering, and people passing who smiled and nodded. He nodded in return. His heavily wrinkled forehead began to soften.

The Brougham had been parked half a block away from the apartment building. As Bob walked down the steps, the car moved up to the entrance, and he got in. "How'd it go?"

"Same old," Bob replied, and opened the purse, fishing out the eight one hundred dollar bills and handing them to Ronald. "I sure can use some smack."

Ronald counted the money and added it to the roll in his left front pants pocket. "I mean, how did they like you as Roberta?"

"They thought the dress and the underwear was cool, real cool," Bob answered, in his monotone voice. "They said they wanted me back again next week."

"Well, all right. We must have been a hit."

"Ronald, I really am starting to feel sick. I need a fix."

"We'll be at the hotel in ten minutes." Ronald passed him a bag of White. "So tell me, were these guys okay to you?"

"Yeah. Each of them came twice with me and maybe twice again with each other. It was just sex, no rough stuff. They told me they had a good time."

"Regular clientele, that's what we want. Steady money."

"Ronald, I don't feel good. Can we hurry back home?"

"Hang tough Bob, you'll be home and high in ten more minutes. How do the clothes feel?"

"They feel different. I feel kind of different when I'm wearing them."

"What do you mean different?"

"Different. Like, like a girl."

"What do you mean, like a girl?"

"I feel like a girl."

"Is that a problem?"

"No, it's just kind of different. People treat me different. I feel like I'm different, like I'm a female."

"And?"

"It's kind of like, softer, gentler. It's kind of cool."

"I'll send Enna out for some more clothes tomorrow," Ronald said to himself. "It seems that we have a gold mine here. This one is going to work out real well."

Charles changed gears after work. The people he worked with during the day did not become his personal friends in the evening. Occasionally he would stop off for a glass of wine or a single drink with them, before heading home. A couple of the staff thought of him as being a little too aloof, because of it. There was very little sharing of his private life with them. Eventually it became an accepted fact that he had his own tight circle of friends and stayed within that group for socializing.

He was single and lived in a stylish and expensive apartment three blocks from the Senator's office. The three-year-old Chevrolet he owned rarely moved from the underground garage during the weekdays, as he always walked to and from. An obvious thing about him was that he wore expensive, expertly tailored clothes. But beyond these few things, nothing was known about him, except for his competence in the day-to-day things related to work. He was purely professional. Only the Senator knew anything of his background.

Without appearing too forward, two of the females on staff did some probing, mainly to find out his actual marital status. From hurried looks into his personnel file, they discovered that he filed taxes singularly and without dependents. Three reference letters praised him for his abilities, intelligence, and work ethic. A fourth reference letter was from a Colonel Waters, Army Intelligence, expounding on Captain Charles Armarin's competence and loyalty. Surprisingly, there was nothing else in the folder. They reasoned that since Phillbroom had hired the man directly, perhaps there was an additional folder in the Senators own files, which he kept locked when he wasn't in his office. The two conspirators were pleased by their meager findings. They had at least confirmed that he was single, and they now knew something more of his background. They were temporarily satisfied.

Enna was sent shopping again. She had made her own list,

determined by budgeting the cash Ronald had given her. The first stop was for two medium priced, but substantially marked down, dresses. One was bright blue silk with long sleeves that flowed all the way to the floor; the other was red chiffon and came to mid thigh. Both were meant to be tight and clingy. The second stop was at a boutique that specialized in sexy party clothes. She found a stretch, demi cup, front lace up bra in red, with a matching stretch, front lace up garter belt, and a blue bustier complete with adjustable garter straps. Enna also purchased red, blue and black hose. She was twenty dollars over budget, but she paid for the purchases anyway. Ronald would reimburse her later. These things were perfect for the job at hand. Like magic, they would transform Bob into Roberta just by putting them on. In the right light, with the hormones flowing, they would move some men to do things they never dreamed of doing before, of taking steps into heightened sexual arousal, compatibility and satisfaction that was accelerated by the implied blatant sexuality of the garments. As Enna said, "they moved the mind." As Ronald said, "they made money."

Ronald's phone grew noticeably busier. Word of mouth about a fresh cross-dresser face circulated rapidly. The flat personality was taken to mean obedience, or coolness, and had no adverse effect on Roberta's popularity. Those who had tried her once found they wanted her back. She could handle group sex as competently as she handled a single partner. It was the groups that requested her most often. There was nothing Roberta wouldn't do or attempt to do. She was always discrete, clean, shaven, wore stunningly sexy clothes, and was on time. She added considerably to Ronald's reputation for having one of the best quality stables of party ponies in New Orleans. This reputation was reflected in Ronald's prices. The prices were never questioned. The quality of clientele was controlled by Ronald. Questionable and overflow requests for outcalls were channeled to other pimps by him. It was becoming very apparent that the kinky stuff was the real moneymaker. Bob, now in his fourth week equaled the income of two of the straight-sex girls. And, Ronald had worked him only three nights a week, one or two gigs a night.

Bob, when he wasn't working, stayed stoned most of the time. The quality of the China White was the best. It took only four hits a day to keep him comfortable. Ronald had bought him a small television set. When he wasn't on the nod, he would watch it. Very often, the set stayed on all day long, as he slept through the programming.

Intellectual pursuits had never been a strong drive in him. These days, the term, "intellectual pursuits," was a puzzle to him. Anything that needed more than cursory thought was dismissed as too difficult. What past he recalled, and everything before Ronald was now pretty hazy, and he didn't go very deep into why's or wherefores. The immediate body needs tagged to physical effects of the heroin, especially the pleasure, dictated his life and commanded the space not taken up in his thoughts by work.

Bob was still confused by the pleasant way he was treated when he worked. The amount of respect, especially when he was dressed in female clothing, made him a little uncertain of what to do or say. Fortunately, the clients usually had in mind exactly what they wanted. He just went along with it.

The female clothing, moreover, made him feel different. When he wore them, he could almost see himself as a girl sometimes. It made him feel softer. A sense of sexuality, long diminished by low self worth and heavy drug use, lightly awakened. The awakening was associated with wearing the dresses and the female underclothes. The response he got from others when he wore them was the most positive show of personal worth he had ever experienced. The way people looked at him, spoke to him, and touched him, when he wore the clothes, was the kindest and the most respectful that he could remember. They made him feel, at least to a small degree, acceptable again. He began to feel happier when he dressed in the clothes.

Enna noticed the difference in him. She applied the makeup, did the hair, and helped dress him, on the days when he had work. She credited change of diet, along with the vitamin intake, for the change. He was showing signs of rising above the hazy shell. It was more noticeable on the days when he worked. He seemed to take a greater interest in how he looked. She started teaching him to swing his hips when he walked in heels. He seemed to pay more attention. He was more aware. He took longer, more careful looks in the mirror when dressing. There was no question about it, Bob enjoyed being a girl.

Word about his drinking had gotten out. Hamilton's secretary had noticed the boozy breath for the fourth morning in a row. The odor of scotch lingered heavily in his office as well, that morning, from a spill the night before. She whispered this choice bit of gossip to her friend in Accounts, with the recommendation that it stay between them. Somehow, it was hinted to the Head of Accounts payable. He, in turn, told his wife.

"The poor man must be in agony over the loss of his friends," they all said, wondering just how far this thing would go. He had always been the stable one, the rock. He was almost like a father to those who worked for him. Now, they all looked for a chink in his armor, a slip in his work habits, or for some reason to be able to say, "Yea, I saw that. Just this afternoon too. Poor man!" But, during work hours he showed no change in personality or work quality. He made things happen, just as he always had. Hamilton was a man who truly enjoyed working, and it showed. There was no apparent change. Still, they watched.

Friday afternoon, Hamilton stayed late, just as he usually did. At a quarter of seven, he put his pen down, brought up the screen saver on his PC monitor, and walked over to the wet bar to open another bottle of J and B. It was number three for the week. He usually didn't nip before it went into the club soda and ice, but the thought of the fresh unadulterated taste of whiskey appealed. He poured two fingers and took a sip. It was at room temperature and tasted great. Flavors that were hidden in the cold clung to his tongue. It was like a different drink. It tasted better than anticipated.

Hamilton eased his medium frame onto the small leather sofa that made up a part of his office furniture, and stretched out his legs onto the other cushion. He took another sip, this time swirling the liquid around in his mouth, then slowly swallowing it. Sitting the glass down on the carpet in front of the sofa, he clasped his hands in back of his head. "What in the world is eating at me," he asked himself? "Have I forgotten some detail? It isn't like me to do that. Since the shellfish incident I haven't been myself, really. Those people had to go. They were good Christian soldiers, they would have understood their sacrifice. That was just a part of this guerrilla action. It was necessary. That can't be the problem. Business is still very good. There are the usual problems, but they are being handled. What is troubling me?" He took up the glass and had another long sip.

Gertrude could hear the phone ringing as she slid the key into the deadbolt lock. Why wouldn't it open? Why did the damned thing screw up when she was out in the hall with her phone ringing? She pushed the key home again, and wiggled it slightly. The lock gave. The doorknob lock opened immediately with the first try. The answering machine was answering the phone. "Hello," she said, picking up the handset. The tape stopped.

"Gertrude, It's Harry Phillbroom."

"Harry, hello. Can you hold on for half a second? I've got to close the door."

"Certainly."

She walked back, closed the door, and threw the deadbolt. "Harry, I'm back. How are you?"

"Couldn't be better. Did I interrupt something? Was this a poor time to have called?"

"Heavens no! I just got home from a little after work shopping."

"Am I correct in thinking that you've already eaten?"

"Yes. I ate at the cafe in the department store."

"Well, tomorrow is Saturday, and this is short notice, but I would like to take you out, and talk your arm off over dinner."

"I'd like that Harry, both the food and the talk."

"Can I pick you up at seven?"

"Seven is fine."

"Do you like seafood?"

"You bet I do."

"Well, that's fine, mighty fine. If you give me directions, I'll collect you promptly at seven, tomorrow."

Gertrude gave him the address.

"I sure am looking forward to seeing you, Gertrude."

"This should be an adventure in time for both of us Harry. Thank you for calling."

"See you tomorrow at seven."

"Good night Harry."

"Good night Gertrude."

Gertrude sat in her favorite overstuffed chair. "My God, that was quick," she said out loud. "I guess we'll have just that much more to chat about when we get together." She got up, went to the kitchen, opened the door to a wine-rack, drew out a bottle of Stag's Leap Merlot and poured a small portion into a wine glass. Settling back into the chair, she took off her shoes, and pulled her classy legs up and over one of the arms. Her stomach tingled. It had been a while since she had accepted a date over the phone. "A date? My God, a date? At my age? Cool down a bit. Let's call it a dinner engagement. Yes, that has some propriety."

Phillbroom had exchanged his double-breasted sincere suit look for a single-breasted sincere suit look. The change made no difference in the way he looked. Gertrude, on the other hand, wore an expensive beige pants suit, that emphasized her womanliness. She wore her hair down. "Let me be Veronica Lake tonight," she had said while brushing out the chestnut mane, concealing the left side of her face. "No, too restrictive." A happy medium was finally obtained with frantic brushing.

She came to the right height, not quite to his shoulder. Phillbroom guessed that without heels she would be about five foot five. She looked really great. He noticed she turned heads, both male and female, as they were escorted to their table. She radiated charm and vibrancy that filled the entire room. Her special, fluid walk brought nods and smiles as they passed. He was very pleased to be with seen with her.

She had had a little tingle in her stomach when he came for her. She felt eighteen. The skin care she had practiced her entire life now provided her with a face that looked twenty years younger than her actual age. She would be sixty-four in a month, but tonight she felt eighteen, and looked, maybe, forty.

Phillbroom retained his driver for the evening. It would be more convenient if he didn't have to worry about having a cocktail or two, or parking, and so forth. He also didn't mind showing off a little. However, he asked to be driven in the lower profile Chevy Caprice and not the Cadillac. Like the single-breasted suit, he thought it made him seem less severe. He was aware that sometimes his presence intimidated people. Tonight, he promised, he would soften himself. He knew how to do it. For certain, he had a gentler side to offer.

Over cocktails they caught up with the happenings in their respective lives between nineteen forty-four and nineteen forty-six. He began by telling her how he had tried to phone her before being shipped out to Chicago. She explained about staying with a girl friend and getting home later that evening. He told about being in training at Fort Ord, near Monterey, for amphibious assault training when the war ended. She and her girlfriend went to Time Square and joined the partying crowd there, dancing, and hugging everyone, and getting kissed hard on the mouth by a sailor. The kiss was so hard and long that it traumatized her lips for nearly an hour. They just buzzed.

Their conversation flowed freely. The intellect of their conversation showed them evenly matched. Anecdote followed anecdote. Humor fitted humor. There was much in common. A friendship was immediately established.

Phillbroom thought to himself how pleased he was that he

didn't intimidate her as he had others. She treated him like a person and not a Senator. It made it easy to relax and be himself. She handled herself so well, so gracefully. My God, but she was charming!

Gertrude wondered if she was being too talkative? But it seemed that what was coming out intuitively worked. And his half of the conversation was so interesting; she was stimulated to move the interchange in his direction for his immediate input. She liked his solid intellect, and the way he put thoughts into words. She really liked Harry, period.

Chapter 11

"Then Try This!"

"Kogi is furious again. Nothing new there. That son of a bitch is always pissed at something, the tight assed bastard," Rendel Schultz said to himself. "What he'd like best would be for me to jump in front of a very fast moving freight train, in front of the TV cameras with explosives strapped around my body. The man wants more blood than I'm willing to give." This was in response to a fax sent to Schultz from Kogi through his intermediary. Kogi felt that there wasn't enough follow up immediately after the last two dealerships were hit. He had expected a full-hearted campaign in Berkeley, which would trigger similar work in other designated cities across the U.S., Berkeley would be the flagship of the KILL THE BILL television efforts. Kogi wanted action. He was paying for action NOW! Do it NOW. Get it organized NOW. Schultz knew Kogi was right. It just bothered him that Kogi never approached him in a positive way, it was always with negative vibes. Schultz knew, or at least had heard, that The 'Coalition' was about to be hit with a Restraining Order, in addition to the two law suit's that had been already been filed against them. Once the Restraining Order was served, they were tied up and of no use. Schultz, therefore was keeping a low profile, and on the move. There was another rumor that the Dealer Association had a put a price on his head or had hired some heavies to personally do a number on him at the next demonstration. He had been through adversity before with demonstration groups. But it was usually the police, whose moves were predictable, not like those of a hit squad.

The Coalition might very well get dusted by the Law. That didn't make any difference to the mother organization, which would just pull another name out of the air from another group and put them back into action. If that happened, Schultz knew that he would certainly not be retained to lead the new group.

Everyone was, it seemed, out to kick his ass. He made up his mind to at least go down fighting. He knew that some of the heavier-duty guys in his group were ready to bust somebody after the mechanics had made them look bad on TV. Schultz made up a fax to send to the intermediary, telling Kogi that a major campaign would shortly be getting underway.

The headlines read, "Senator Maurice Hillby Dies In A One Car Accident. Senator Hillby who was a guest speaker yesterday at the Aspen Institute, died when his car left the highway in Glenwood Canyon and rolled two hundred feet down a slope and into the boulders along the Colorado River early this morning. A spokesperson for the Colorado

State Patrol said it appeared that Senator Hillby lost control of his car on a curve and went off the roadway. No skid marks were found indicating that he may have fallen asleep at the wheel."

Satchel looked up from a desk full of data that he was entering into his computer. "Humm, reading while walking. Not a great talent, but talent. What could cause you to throw caution to the wind and attempt to wander into my office without looking," he asked of Hansen?

Hansen took no notice of the humor. "Take a look at this," he said, laying the newspaper down over the material on Satchels desk.

"Oh, my gosh. Hillby!"

"One down, and how many left to go," Hansen asked?

Satchel pulled his glasses off and looked up at Hansen. "You aren't thinking what I think you are thinking?"

"Why not?"

"Well, why?"

"This is a very convenient situation. It was a one car accident, no one in the car but him."

"Why is being alone in the car out of place?"

"Satch, this guy lives a few miles away in Vail. If you were going to Aspen overnight do you think you could escape taking your wife or sixteen-year-old daughter? Especially when the tab is being picked up? The answer is no."

"Hey, maybe his wife was away shopping, along with the daughter."

"Satch, if you read the article, you'll see that she was at home when the sheriff reached her with the news."

"Bill, that just means that she didn't ride back to Vail with him. I think you're reading a bit more into this than is actually there. Jesus, you're another Perry Mason." Satchel grinned.

"My intuition is running the show here, Satch, that's true. But take a look at the overall view. One, the Senator knows the road. He lives near by. Two, the accident occurred at about seven in the evening. It's still light in Colorado, at seven, this time of the year. Three, he didn't try to stop the car, just drove off the road. Four, the man is renowned tea-totaler. Booze can pretty well be ruled out. Five, he's a married man who would normally have his wife with him for a trip to Aspen." "Wives just don't let their husbands go to Aspen alone, not with all that shopping potential."

"Bill, that's not reason enough to throw any suspicion on this event. It just isn't. The man got sleepy and drove off the road. End of story. It happens every day, even to bright, non-drinking Senators from Colorado."

"Satchel, I tell you this guy left the highway and wound up in the boulders beside the Colorado River, but not because he fell asleep and drove off the road."

"Well, Sherlock, you are going to have to prove it."

"All right, you're on." Hansen walked back into his office and immediately picked up the phone and dialed. "Yes, Information? Give me the number for the Pitkin County Sheriff's Office. Thanks." "Pitkin County Sheriff." "Hello, I would like to speak with Sheriff Assa Albin." "I'll connect you." "Albin here."

"Assa, this is Bill Hansen."

"Bill, like a bolt out of the blue. Haven't talked to you since February at the Red Onion. How the devil are you?"

"Oh, so you do remember being in the Red Onion, on or about eight in the evening, February twenty-fourth, and drinking a full bottle of Linea Aquavit? Remember anything else?"

"Yeah, I remember never to beat you in a race down Ajax again. My head still hurts from that night. Winning sure isn't everything it's cracked up to be."

"Assa, I'll give you another chance next February."

"I'll loose! You may as well know in advance. I swear, I just couldn't go through winning again."

"Admit it Assa, if you had to push me off Ruthie's Run and into the boulders below the last shoulder, you'd do it, just to win."

"Into the boulders, huh? Well, you're making me weaken, you smooth talkin' city boy."

Hansen smiled into the mouthpiece, "And speaking of boulders, tell me about the Senator."

"Why you rascal. You blind-sided me on that one. I never saw it coming."

"I'm sorry to be so abrupt. I'm looking for some information on Senator Hillby's accident."

"Bill, that accident actually took place just inside the Eagle County line, near Dotsero. But if you want me to, I'll call and get an accident report, and send it to you."

"That would be terrific, but it may not be necessary. In confidence, is there any scuttlebutt around about it?"

"Well, strictly between us, okay?"

"Certainly, just between us."

"The Coroner over there thinks that there may be one too many prangs on this guy's head. Now that sure as hell isn't for publication yet. He's still making measurements. The Senator was driving a convertible, so that prang may be up for grabs.

How many rocks did his head bounce off of?" "Do you know if he was wearing a seat belt?"

"Oh yes, he was belted. And the air bags even deployed."

"So he landed upside down?"

"Yeah, after a couple of rolls, the car stopped upside down beside the river. I'm surprised it didn't burn."

"Why are you surprised? All of these later cars have a fuel

shutoff that works when the car turns upside down."

"I know about that, of course. But this car didn't have a fuel cap and gas was flung all over the place. In fact, the tank drained while it was upside down, with a lot of the gas flowing over the side of the car and into the interior."

"Those gas caps are screw-in type, and there's a flapper valve in the tank inlet neck that keeps the gas in on a roll-over."

"Screw-in or not, the cap wasn't on or anywhere near the car, and the flapper wasn't working. Whoever put gas in, the last time, probably didn't put the cap back on. Happens every day. And the flapper is mechanical, it could have failed."

"Could be."

"Why so interested, Bill?"

"I knew him. We worked on some things together."

"Your curiosity seems a bit on the high side. You know something they don't know in Eagle?"

"I don't have anything concrete."

"That might imply that you have something not concrete," Assa's grin could be felt through the phone.

"Assa, I'm thinking of taking a few days off. How about me dropping in to see you?"

"I might buy you a burger and a beer."

"Then that settles it. I'll see you in a few days."

"Do you want me to get you a room?"

"No, not yet. I think I'll go into Eagle airport. I may drop a fly into that stretch of water just before the canyon. Maybe stay locally for a day or two."

"Does that mean that you want me to call the Sheriff up there and tell him you're going to call on him?"

Hansen laughed, "Yeah, if it will make you feel any better."

"Okay Bud, see you when you get here. By the way, the Eagle County Sheriff is Sam Goddard."

"Thanks Assa. See you in a few days."

Hansen walked into Greens office. "Do you think you can handle it for a week or so without me. I want to go to Colorado."

"It will probably take that long for me to gather all the data we need for Norske Fisk. There is nothing critical, that I know of, that hits us with any deadline for a while."

"Okay, pencil me off the calendar starting tomorrow. I'll leave some phone numbers with Gertrude. No, better yet, I'll just call with the phone number when I get there."

"Going to Aspen?"

"Eventually. But I'll probably be flying into Eagle first."

"They have phones in Eagle Colorado?"

"Really Satchel, there is life beyond Chesapeake Bay."

"Couldn't prove it by me. But I guess your time off has something to do with Hillby?"

"I'm going to make a quick pass at that situation, then go fishing with Assa."

"Are you taking the Beechcraft or going commercial?"

"It will be a lot of flying, but I really enjoy flying that old plane, so, I'll take it. That's predicated on the weather, of course. If it looks like it can be done VFR, the Beech and I are out of here tomorrow morning."

"Taking anyone along?"

"No, just me and my autopilot."
"Well, watch those mountains out west. I understand there are a lot of airplane parts scattered throughout Colorado."

Hansen grinned," What a grim send off this is Satch."

"Well, just be careful, like I know you'll be, Bill." Hansen noted that Satchel was quietly serious.

"Most aviation accidents happen when pilots who are inexperienced with high altitudes fly into those altitudes expecting sea level performance from their airplanes. And they usually do it in marginal weather or when there are high winds. I don't do any of those three. Pork Barrel would never forgive me if I bent her."

"Yes, I guess this isn't your first time into Aspen."

"Thanks for your concern Satch. Would you like to go along and keep an eye on me?"

"You know how I hate flying. Big planes, small planes, it doesn't matter, I dislike them both. Flying is unnatural." This Satchel said with a perfectly straight face and without looking up from the material on his desk.

Hansen put a hand on Satchels shoulder, "I'm headed home to pack and put together a flight plan. See you then, in a week or ten days or whenever."

Satchel looked up, pulled his reading glasses down on his nose, and smiled, "Do have a splendid vacation, Bill."

Hansen stopped just long enough to fill Gertrude in on his plans, then vanished out through the double glass doors of the office.

Chapter 12

"Gone Fishing"

Pork Barrel and it's pilot had spent the following night at North Platte. The motel's shuttle driver picked Hansen up at Butler Aviation's lounge, and took him the short distance to the motel. After stashing his overnight bag in the room, he immediately headed for the restaurant and that huge Nebraska melt-in-your-mouth T-bone he'd been dreaming about since he left the airport traffic pattern in Washington. He was coyote hungry. Two cups of coffee, from the trusty thermos, and two sandwiches eaten over Columbus had totally worn off over Des Moines.

There were no weather fronts en route, with the only clouds being fair weather cumulus. Moderate chop had lasted for only the last hour. The flight to this point had had one fuel stop and was picture perfect.

The next stage of the flight terminated at Jeffco airport,

northwest of Denver. Here Hansen would have the option of renting a car and continuing by road, if the weather in the Rockies was poor, or flying the Beech across the Continental divide and into Eagle if the weather was good. This stage began at zero five-thirty the following morning, with those two old Pratt and Whitney radial engines breaking the morning silence when they barked themselves awake.

Hansen lived for the takeoff runs in this airplane. This morning, with lots of runway available at this ex-military training base, he deliberately took more time to come to takeoff power when he started the run. The plane was well above minimum single engine control speed when it flew itself off using less than a third of the runway with one notch of flaps. Hansen trimmed for a three hundred foot per minute climb as he left the airport pattern. It was a cloudless day. The sun was just now touching the taller towers. This was going to be another fine flying day.

"You slime ball son-of-a-bitch, you scum bag asshole, you low-life motherfucker, you shit eater, get out of that fuckin' bed right now or I'll break your fuckin' neck!" Ronald grabbed the covers on Bob's bed and flung them onto the floor.

"Oh Ronald, I'm so tired man. I just can't go anywhere right now."

Ronald grabbed Bob by the hair on the back of his neck and jerked him out of bed. Bob went onto his knees. The tears flowed from his eyes.

"Ow, oh shit that hurts. Stop. Stop pulling my hair." Bob

broke down and cried openly. Ronald gave the hair another vicious jerk then let go.

Ronald looked like he wanted to kick his guts in. "Listen to me you no good cocksucker. You get into that bathroom and get cleaned up, before I throw you out that fuckin' window. Do it now!"

"Ronald, honest to God, I'm sick, I've got stomach cramps. I hurt all over. I just can't go out tonight."

Ronald slapped him real hard twice, then waded into him. Bob rolled into a fetal position to protect himself, but he still felt the sting of the blows all over his body. Ronald had completely lost it. Bob was screaming as he was kicked until a thrust knocked the wind out of him, and he passed out. Blood flowed out of his nose and from his mouth. Large welts were beginning to form on his arms and torso. Ronald stopped with the beating only after he finally realized there was no noise coming out of Bob.

"You sack of shit. After all I've done for you, you aren't going to fuck me over. You owe me. Do you understand what I'm telling you, you owe me?" Bob didn't move.

Roland brought a glass of water from the bathroom and threw it in Bob's face. The downed man groaned, and moved an arm to a cover position over his face. At that moment, a key entered the lock, the door opened and Enna walked in.

"Whoa! What do we have here?" She could feel the rage radiating from Ronald, and saw Bob on the floor. Bob groaned again. Enna stooped down and touched Bob on the shoulder, "Is there a little problem going on?" Bob shuddered and tightened into a ball at her touch.

"This asshole won't get up for work," Ronald looked as if he might start in on Bob again, but instead, took one step back.

"Bob!" Enna gently touched him again. "Bob, it's Enna. Bob, why don't you want to go to work?"

"I'll tell you why he didn't want to go to work," Ronald's anger was peaking again, "because he's getting too fucking lazy to get out of bed." With that he aimed another vicious kick at Bob's midsection, which was absorbed mostly by Bob's arms. Bob screamed!

"Holy Jesus, Ronald. Stop, you're gonna hurt him bad."

Ronald stood over Bob menacingly. "He isn't going to fuck with me. I'm going to teach him or kill him."

Enna placed herself on the floor between them, kneeling beside Bob and pulling him up to a sitting position. "Roland, you've given him enough. Shit, just look what you've done to him. How will I ever get him fixed up enough to send him out the door?"

"Enna, I don't care what you do with him, just have him the ready to work by nine." Ronald had stopped yelling. He walked to the door, turned and before he closed it said, "Have him at the curb at nine. If I have to come back up here again tonight, I'll kill him."

"Come on Bob, get your feet back under you. We need to

get you up on the bed for a little bit." Enna's nursing training was tested getting his naked body off the floor and onto the bed. He was limp as a rag, and groaned as she deposited him on the bed.

She shook her head as she took inventory of the marks Ronald had left. Coming back from the bathroom with a wet and a dry towel, she began cleaning his face. Bob seemed a little dazed, but no concussion was apparent. The bloody nose could be cleaned up, as well as the split lip. There were going to be a lot of big bruises to cover. Makeup probably wouldn't take care of all of them. Some were coloring in dark as she looked at him. "Guess I'll just sponge you off. I don't want you running hot water over that body just yet. How do you feel, hon?"

"Enna, I'm sick, really sick. I think I got the flu."

"When did you shoot up last?"

"About three hours ago, I think."

Enna found one of Ronald's little plastic bags of smack on the desk. He must have dropped it by for Bob's use tonight," she thought. "I'll shoot him up with part of this stuff. It will take the pain away at least. So maybe I can get him glued together enough to make the show tonight. For certain he's going to go to work." She prepared half the bag of heroin and shot him up.

The warmth flowed through his body. Everything was soothed. The cramping in his stomach stopped, the places where he was kicked and hit didn't hurt anymore. He felt wonderful, and was only slightly aware of someone stroking his body with an alcohol filled sponge. He couldn't keep his eyes open.

Enna had done the best she could. The face was made up heavier than normal, using foundation and camouflage cream. The bruises on his arms and body would have to be covered with clothing. She chose the black mid-thigh dress with long sleeves. Tonight Roberta would have a couple of extra sprays of Chanel. It would keep the illusion alive longer. Instructions would be to keep the clothing on if possible. The abdomen and arms were a mess, along with the face. But at least Roberta would be there at the curb at nine when Ronald rolled up.

Jefferson County Airport tower approved a straight in approach. Hansen went through his descent checklist, bringing the power back and trimming the nose up to a one-twenty approach speed. He reached to the right side of the console to add a notch of flaps, the indicator on the panel stopped at fifteen degrees.

At three miles, he proceeded with the landing checklist. His hand on the landing gear switch brought the gear down, he then added fifteen degrees more flaps, and re-trimmed, props placed at fine pitch. A scan of the engine instruments indicated everything was okay. The Pratt and Whitney's purred with a softer tone. The tower cleared the Beechcraft to land.

A mile out Hansen added the last fifteen degrees of flaps, brought the power back again, and trimmed the airplane for touchdown. A minor crosswind required a little cross control to keep the Beech's nose straight down the runway.

He wheel landed the plane just beyond the numbers, working the rudder pedals briskly in order to keep it moving straight, and slowly brought the tail down.

Hansen took the first taxiway off the runway. The tower cleared him to ground control frequency. Ground control cleared him to the ramp. Opening the cowl flaps, he taxied to a tie down area near the small terminal.

It was sunny and warm, but the wind felt a little stronger than the ten knots the tower had advised. At more than a mile above sea level, the air was always dryer here. The eighty-degree temperature felt like seventy back in D.C.

The Weather Service had seven pilot reports for the route and altitude Hansen intended to fly to Eagle, indicating headwinds of about twenty knots, with light to moderate chop. Winds aloft were forecast not to increase. Cloud cover to remain less than three- tenths for the next forty-eight hours. It was a definite go. He filed his VFR flight plan to Eagle County Airport. The fuel truck arrived just as Hansen arrived back at the Beech.

He disliked the oxygen mask, but put it on after climbing through twelve thousand feet, en route to crossing the Continental Divide near Loveland Pass at fourteen thousand five hundred.

Dillon Reservoir's deep blue depths contrasted with the pine and spruce covered slopes undulating down to the waters edge. Visibility was over one hundred miles in the dry, light air. Hansen, who was essentially following I-70 westward, could see the pattern of ski slopes at Copper Mountain which were in the light green of grasses and wild flowers contrasting with the darker conifers.

As the ski slopes of Vail passed below, Hansen started his descent into Eagle airport. Over Wolcott he called Eagle's tower requesting a straight in approach. Eagle tower advised him to enter the landing pattern at midfield, as they had two other aircraft already in pattern. The Beech was on the ground six minutes later.

After refueling the plane and topping off the oil tanks, Hansen unlashed his overnight bag, another bag of fishing gear, and a suitcase from the front right passenger seat. A phone call had brought the motel shuttle to the airport. He made one more pass through the cockpit to make sure the control locks were in place and the master switch was off. Through the windshield he saw the shuttle pull up, and the driver get out and open the rear door, getting ready to receive the luggage. Hansen locked the cabin door, checked the tie down chains again, then picked up his suitcase and the bags and walked to the waiting van. "Hi, I'm Bill."

"Welcome to Eagle, Bill," the driver said. "Let me have those bags."

On the ride to town, the driver asked Hansen if this was his first time in Eagle. "No, I get out here once or twice a year, and I've stayed several times in your town. I like to fish the Colorado and the Eagle Rivers. I've hunted a couple of times near Bond."

"You must know the area like a native."

"I lived at Vail for three years after it opened back in the sixties. I got to know this area pretty well, roamed it in a nineteen fifty-five Volkswagen Bus."

"You've got me beat, Bill. I've only been here two years, myself. I went bust in a pizza place over in Grand Junction. My brother-in-law is a contractor here, in town. He put a roof over my head and gave me part time work for a while. He split to work on a project near Telluride. I stayed and got on with the motel. By the way, my name's Pete."

"Pleased to meet you Pete," Hansen said.

"Likewise. So you staying long?"

"Probably two or three days, I'd like to do a little fishing."

"The fishing hasn't been the best this year. But I heard there have been some limits taken above Minturn."

"I have a few places I'll be trying while I'm here."

Pete smiled," I take it they'll go unnamed?"

"If I score, I'll let you know about them, maybe." Hansen smiled.

The van stopped at the motel entrance, Pete unloaded the baggage and insisted on carrying it into the lobby. "Many thanks, Pete." Hansen tried to palm some ones into Pete's hand."

"No you don't. You're not getting off that easy." Hansen's jaw dropped. "If you score, you've got to tell me where those secret holes are," Pete said going from dead serious to a grin.

Hansen collected himself and returned the humor. "I might share one of them, if I'm wildly successful, and I mean WILDLY successful."

"Millie, be sure and give Mr. Hansen here the quietest room in the place, I want him to get plenty of rest so he can concentrate on fishing," Pete vocalized.

Hansen smiled to himself, it was good to see that Denver hadn't completely crept over the mountains. There was still an open, western personality alive in the people of Eagle in spite of the urbanization at the eastern end of the county. Every year more sprawl was added, it appeared. Ranches were falling one by one in retreat. He wondered how many more years it would be until this beautiful valley was completely swallowed by condos and expensive homes, and the sight of cattle grazing along side the highway would be lost forever. There were just too many people in this world. It was causing too many changes. The loss of agricultural land involved in these changes made him feel uncomfortable. He was tired from the flying, but the thoughts added sadness to the tiredness making him melancholy at three in the afternoon.

He called the car rental. They said they would bring a midsize Chevy wagon to the motel. Hanging clothes and organizing toilet articles busied him until the rental car arrived. After which, he jumped into a super hot shower, that helped brighten the already sunny afternoon.

"Eagle County Sheriff." A female voice, probably the dispatcher Hansen thought, answered on the first ring.

"Good afternoon. My name is Bill Hansen. I'd like to speak

to Sheriff Goddard."

"Just a moment please."

A deeper female voice came on the line. "This is Deputy Dawgler, may I help you?"

"Deputy Dawgler," Hansen repeated the name to help him remember it, "this is Bill Hansen. I'd like to speak to Sheriff Goddard."

"Mister Hansen, the Sheriff told me to expect your call. He had to be out of the office this afternoon. He will probably return late tonight."

"Does he work tomorrow?"

"Normally he takes the weekends off, but he asked me to tell you he'll be happy to meet anybody, any time and any day of the week, who can give Assa Albin a three day hangover. I guess your reputation is preceding you, Mr. Hansen."

"It sounds like the Sheriff of Pitkin County has been telling stories out of school."

"It didn't necessarily make the newspapers, but it was the talk of us Law Enforcement folks for a month. Poor Assa took a heck of a ribbing on that one."

"He never should have beaten me in that race. I'm clearly a much faster skier. He must have cheated, probably waxed his skis or something loathful like that."

The Deputy laughed. "It would be just like him to pull something like that, wouldn't it?"

"You did say a three day hangover, didn't you," Hansen quipped.

The Deputy roared, "Yep!" Her laughter finally died to a snigger. "Do you want me to have the Sheriff call you when he gets back, Mister Hansen?"

"If he returns before ten, I'd appreciate a call. If he doesn't, a call tomorrow will work out just as well, I suppose."

"Okay, Mister Hansen, I'll tell him or leave a message for him. It was sure nice talking to you."

"Thanks for your help Deputy."

"Any time. Have a good afternoon."

Hansen hung up wishing he had inquired of the whereabouts of Hillby's wrecked car, perhaps gotten a look at it this afternoon. The Deputy seemed amiable enough, but it would probably be better if he initiated any inquiry about the Hillby case through the Sheriff himself. Obviously, Assa had already spoken to Goddard about his interest. He hoped that Goddard would be as open with him as he knew Assa would be under similar circumstances.

Hansen's phone rang at nine-thirty. "Mr. Hansen, this is Sam Goddard."

"Sheriff Goddard. Thanks for calling."

"I hope I'm not calling too late."

"Not at all."

"Assa said you were interested in the Hillby accident."

"Yes I am. I wonder if I might chat with you about it. Say, tomorrow, if possible?"

"How about breakfast, eight-o-clock, there at your motel's coffee shop?"

"Terrific, see you then. And thank you."

"Have a nice evening."

"Thanks Sheriff. Good night."

Charles worked late again. Usually he worked in one of his Armani Double Breasted suits, but this evening the jacket was off and folded over the back of a chair. He was working in his shirtsleeves. Phillbroom passed his office, stopped, then put his head in the door opening. "Still at it I see. If it can wait until tomorrow, come on along. I'll buy you one for the road." And then with humor, he added, "You are still walking, aren't you?"

"Hi Senator. I am trying to tie up some loose ends so we can get away on that fishing trip the day after tomorrow. Afraid I'll have to take a rain check on that drink."

"If it will guarantee that we get away, by all means work as late as you like. I'll see you in the morning. Good night."

"Good night Harry," he said to Phillbroom, and then to himself he said, "Jesus, that was too close, way too close. I didn't think anyone was still here, let alone him. I was lucky to have heard him coming along the hallway." He uncovered the Rolodex, he had removed from Phillbroom's desk, from under the folded jacket. Hurriedly he finished copying the last of the selected names, addresses, and phone numbers onto the P.C. screen, and then hit Print.

When Schultz saw the man point the gun at him, he immediately hit the ground. He thought he actually heard the bullets go past him. Three loud reports with maybe a second between each, echoed off the walls in front of the Saturn dealership. He stayed flattened until he heard the screeching of tires from a car accelerating away from the scene. Only then did he get to his feet. "Shit," he yelled, as he looked down at the wetness on the front of his trousers. He had pissed his pants.

The instinct to save his own life had been so intense that he hadn't heard the screams of the frightened demonstrators as they also dived to the ground. Amazingly, no one was hurt. The police and the TV news truck arrived at the same time.

"Just where the fuck were you," Schultz screamed at Glen Glege, "some asshole took a shot at me."

"There was an accident on the Bay Bridge, traffic was a bitch. Wait! Did you say someone took a shot at you?" Asked Glege, with disbelief.

"Yeah, I saw the guy actually pointing the gun at me. Fuck! That was no joke. I damn near got killed one minute ago."

Glege motioned to the cameraman to start filming just as two policemen walked up.

The evening news segment from Berkeley brought a small smile from Kogi, "There now, we're back on the screen. This should keep us there for a couple of weeks."

He had not been home in the evenings, going on fourteen days. The office had now superseded his home. Hamilton had always maintained a small assemblage of clothes in the closet of the dressing room that was attached to his personal restroom. A shower was built into the restroom providing the executive complete amenities. A French laundry picked up and delivered to the business address, at discrete hours. A case of J and B Scotch, and two cases of Schweppes Club Soda were likewise delivered well after working hours.

He was aware that liquor had become a very important part of his evenings, and his life, to the extent that he didn't go out for dinner anymore. Hamilton had even stayed away from the Kiwanis breakfasts, his first absence in nearly twenty years. Food now had a limited appeal. He was down to one meal a day, usually supper, brought in by one of several restaurants that delivered. Scotch consumption was nearly two thirds of a bottle an evening.

What had been a warm, open employee relationship with everyone who worked for him had now deteriorated. Only rarely was his office door open. Although he still had a smile for those who sought his counsel, he didn't wander through the ranks anymore with compliments and encouragement. A man noted for his outward concern for his people, he now rarely spoke with anyone. His reactions weren't as sharp or as precise, as viewed by some. It seemed that he wasn't paying that close of attention to the daily operations. People noticed.

Hamilton, when asked to dinner by friends, begged off, saying, work had piled up and he just couldn't get away. These same friends had been set aside when the religious group was consuming his time. Now they were being rejected again.

Actually, he was beginning to prefer his own company, especially in the evenings, that is, his own company and that of J and B. Day by day, he retreated a little more into himself and his prayers. Jesus would find him an answer.

Chapter 13

"The Fishing"

"Scrambled eggs, bacon, and a short stack," Sheriff Goddard said, in answer to the waitress's question.

"And you sir?" She asked Hansen.

"Make mine a green chili burrito plate."

"Whoa, Bill. You're eatin' like a true Westerner."

"That's because I was raised in Santa Fe, Sam."

"I guess you wouldn't have picked up burrito eatin' in Washington, D.C., would you?"

"I think I imported it back there with me. There are actually two places, near where I live, who now have some Mexican items on their menus. The taste isn't like here in the west, but not bad."

"It's good to see the east hasn't warped your western sensitivities," Sam said.

"I went to Washington twelve years ago. It took a while to adjust to the different style back there, and the way food is prepared. Now I enjoy living and eating back there, but it is always terrific to get west again and enjoy the food and the people. There is no question about it, when I retire, I'll come back west again."

"According to Assa, you get out here often enough now to cause him problems while you're here," Sam laughed.

"Everyone on the western slope must have heard about our après ski race party by now. Poor Assa, he suffered through that win."

"Yeah, he did suffer," Sam smirked. "I think his racial heritage jumped up and bit him with that aquavit. Norway avenged him changing countries."

"Actually, the deal was that the winner got a bottle of Linea Aquavit, but he had to drink it when and where it was served. It was one of those spur of a moment bets we made before starting down Ajax. Kind of high school bravado, I suppose."

"Well, it gave the County something to talk about for a few days anyhow, Bill. We had some good clean American fun at Assa's expense, even up here in Eagle County."

"Deputy Dawgler and I enjoyed the scenario on the phone yesterday, she sounded pretty tickled."

"Around the office she refers to herself as Deputy Dog. If you follow old TV cartoons, you'll appreciate that one. She said the two of you had a fun chat. But I guess you didn't ask her anything about the Senator, because she didn't say anything to me."

"No, I thought it best to go through the proper chain with this. I don't want to create any extra outside interest in the Senator's accident. I would prefer to do nothing that would provoke newspaper interest beyond what has already taken place. My inquiry is personal."

"Assa and I have already talked, as you know. He is comfortable providing you with any information about this case. More importantly, so am I, after meeting you. He also said you may have some information to share as well. Perhaps we can get into things back at the office after breakfast."

"Thanks, Sam. That would be fine."

Sam set the file in front of Hansen, took a seat beside him, then opened the file. There were multiple pictures of the wrecked car, taken at the site where it was found. Some of the pictures were grizzly scenes of the Senator still belted into the overturned car, his arms at odd angles hanging down toward the ground, his face expressionless. In these photos, the deflated air bags also hung out of the dash and steering wheel like giant beige balloons, dangling in front of the corpse's face. There was surprisingly little blood on the man's head. Close up pictures showed what appeared to be half a dozen marks on the baldhead, including one that was longer than the others on the left side, just above the man's ear. "What about this one," Hansen asked?

"Let's go see the Coroner," said Sam.

"Well, Bill, that's the one I'm having trouble with. I don't have all the scientific equipment in the world here in this little corner of the world, but due to the blood flow associated with this longer contusion, I'd say it happened sometime before all the others," said the Coroner. "I really believe that this may have been the blow that killed him, and that it happened before the others. The other contusions and abrasions are consistent with blows from the rocks along the path the car took coming down the hillside."

"Do you think he was hit on the head before the car rolled over," Hansen asked?

"Could have been a Louisville Slugger, or the equivalent."

"I knew it," Hansen said.

Sam looked at Hansen, pushed his Stetson back on his head, and said, "Okay Bill, it looks like it's your turn at bat, no pun intended of course. Whatcha got that's connected here?"

"A possible motive. A possible source for initiation of a hit on the Senator, no pun intended." Hansen filled both men in on the circumstances that he believed might have led to the Senator's death, starting with the turnaround vote on Phillbroom's bill. He described, but did not name Kogi.

"Do you have anything solid that could be used as evidence, Bill?"

"No. I'm running on pure intuition."

"Well," said Sam, "that might not be enough for a jury here in Eagle County to convict with, even though the perpetrator is from out of town. Oh, and by the way, does this suspect have a name?"

"Wow, am I in a spot with that question. I could get my ass kicked if this guy knew that I linked his name with the death of Hillby."

"Bill we don't intend to go running to the API with the name, but, we can quietly investigate if we have the name."

"If this guy is involved, he hired the people to do the job. You can bet he will have covered and distanced himself from the actual event. He has sources. No, he has extraordinary sources and resources."

"Is it the head of the FBI?" Sam smiled.

"No, Sam. His name is Kogi, C.E.O. of Kogi International, Washington, D.C.. And please be very careful with any investigation of him. He has eyes everywhere."

"For the present Bill, there is no reason for the name to go anywhere beyond the three of us. And like you've said, there sure isn't anything we can tag him with, at least not this time. As to the future, we are used to working with what they call in the big cities, high profile people. You have my word, you will not be brought into this thing if it gets hot."

"Thanks Sam."

"Do you still want to see Hillby's car?"

"You bet I do."

"Then let's you and I head on over to Bonner Towing. We'll leave the Coroner here to start an in depth autopsy."

When the Sheriff pulled the blue tarp away from the wrecked car, Hansen was unable to identify the make. He could only discern that it had been a dark blue convertible. The damage was such that it appeared to have rolled several times. There wasn't a single body panel that wasn't damaged. The car reeked of gasoline.

"Speaks for itself, I'd say Bill. Looks to me like it went over twice on the way down, just like the Highway Patrol report says. He had a little overnight bag on the back seat that got flung out on the first roll. We found it midway up the slope. Nothing unusual in the bag. When we found the car it was upside down, as you saw in the Coroner's pictures of the body. It was still in Drive and the ignition was still on. Naturally the engine had stopped because the inertia switch had shut down the fuel flow."

"It's just as I'd pictured. Guess I've seen enough. Let me help you cover it up again, Sam." They brought the tarp over the car and secured it with bungie cords .

"Well, what else would you like to see this morning?"

"Sam, I've looked at everything I care to see regarding Hillby. I think it's time to scout out a couple of my old fishing holes."

"Is Assa coming to join you?"

"No, I'll meet him in a few days in Aspen."

"If you'd like some company, later in the day, there are a couple of holes on the Eagle River, where it runs through my property, that I'd like to show you."

"Oh yes, indeed. What time are you calling it quits?"

"I was thinking of getting away a little early today. You know I worked pretty late last night."

"Sam, you don't need to justify this for me. What time?"

"Pick you up at your motel at four-thirty."

"Gertrude, this is Harry Phillbroom."

"Hi, Harry. It's nice to hear from you."

"Why thank you Gertrude. I am going to be out of town for a few days. I should be back next Friday. Can we get together again, for cocktails and dinner, say, Saturday at six?"

"Cocktails and dinner, next Saturday at six. Let's do it."

"I may have some pretty believable fishing stories to tell you by then."

"This sounds as if a vacation is about to happen to you."

"Yes. I'm getting together with a couple of friends in Louisiana for some bass fishing. We're goin' off the beaten path, out to where the big ones are hidin'."

"When we get together, I'll bring Guinness's Book of World Records, just in case we need it."

"Gertrude, you are a treat."

"Thank you Harry."

"I wish you a pleasant week."

"A fruitful time with the bass, to you."

"Bye Gertrude."

"Good bye Harry." She then to herself," God another one minute telephone conversation with that man. But, he did call me. I'm the one who has been engaged for cocktails and dinner. What am I bitching about? Honest to Pete, Gertrude, sometimes I don't understand you."

Phillbroom's first cast was a beauty. The lure sailed out twenty yards and fell beside the tree stump. There was a flash under water as the bass, running like a torpedo, slammed into the Rebel lure, carrying it upward, exploding the surface of the tranquil bayou. "Will you look at that," the guide exclaimed!

"Dumb luck," Phillbroom grinned back, as he worked the rod and reel, fighting the two and a half pounder back toward the airboat, and the guide's outstretched landing net.

And so it went, for the next four casts, a strike and a fish. Then, it was as if time had been called. You couldn't buy a strike. The Senator even changed plugs. Nothing worked.

There were four boats working nearly half an acre of water. Phillbroom was the only fisherman to connect. This led to some grand fisherman patter back at the camp later. "While you boys were sitting on your asses, I was out there collecting your suppers for tonight. You guys come down here to fish or just beat the water to a froth? Maybe I better take the day off tomorrow so y'all can begin to catch up. Or maybe you guys aught to have your guides run you past the seafood department down at Safeway." Phillbroom spread it on heavy, and enjoyed it. A little later when the five fish had been filleted and grilled, Phillbroom, indeed, provided supper for everyone including the guides.

Before dinner mint juleps loosened the fishing kinks out of those doing the fishing. The guides stayed with a beer each. When seconds on the juleps were announced, Phillbroom switched to whiskey and ditch. His body didn't tolerate the sweet drinks or a lot of alcohol very well any more. He was determined to have a good time without headaches or hangovers.

Charles and Phillbroom's two War buddies each had seconds on the juleps. They were so delicious, and went down easy. Aided by bowls of salted peanuts rolled in ground, dry, hot chili peppers, two drinks turned into three of whatever was being drunk before the dinner bell was rung.

Over food the amiability flowed. The men laughed at each others hard strikes and lost fish, the thrill of going fast in the airboats, the bird's nest in Charles fishing line, and the exploits of other fishing trips and fishermen. Tonight, there was no outside world, not even the hint of one, it was just fishing, and fishermen. There were two cell phones in camp, one that belonged to the chief guide, and one that Charles carried. Neither phone rang. They were turned off.

While out near Dotsero, Colorado, Sam Goddard pointed to a swirl in the current about thirty feet out. "There's a good sized boulder out there, and a hell of a deep hole behind it. When the riffles up stream let you down, or floating a wet fly near the undercut bank up stream doesn't produce, drop a fly in above that swirl and let her drift around twice before she catches the upwelling. I can't promise a strike, but I've personally never fished that hole without a couple of good strikes."

Hansen selected and tied on a light green Willow fly at Sam's suggestion. It took four casts to get line movement that suited him. On the fifth cast, he went for the swirl. The fly made two circuits and started slowly down stream. The big German Brown, his mouth wide open with Hansen's fly in it, shot upwards a foot and a half out of the water. Hansen was so startled he jerked the fly up and away before the fish could clamp his jaws down on it. The bewildered trout quarter rolled and splashed back into the Eagle River. "Damn it."

Sam stifled a belly laugh and slid the sunglasses back up on his nose. "I'd say you could be as selective as you want to be Bill. There's a bunch of fish in this river. Don't just fall for the first one that tries to get on your line. Hell, I agree with your tactics. Make 'em mad. Make 'em hungry."

Hansen smiled sheepishly. "I can't believe I did that," he said. "A real greenhorn exhibition, wasn't it?"

"Happens to every fisherman, Bill. But it's best if it doesn't happen in front of an eye witness who might just blab it all over a three county area by tomorrow afternoon." Sam grinned. "Only kidding Bill. Only kidding. Think I'll head up stream and work those willows near the bridge. Meet you back at the ranch house around seven-thirty for dinner."

"Thanks Sam." Hansen waited until Sam was clear of his casting before he made another try of the swirl.

"Scotch and soda?" Sam handed Hansen a large Kosta double old-fashioned glass, filled with broken ice, the amber colored liquor came a third of the way up the side. "There is a chilled bottle of soda on the sideboard." Sam laid two good-sized New York strips on the grill.

Hansen had just washed up and was putting his fishing gear away in the rented station wagon. The twilight, the co-mingling of smells of pine, sagebrush, the river, and the meadow grasses, and the sweet lightness of the evening air, gave an unmistakable tranquility to the end of the day. The patio of Sam's ranch house with comfortable outdoor furniture, the added smells of beef cooking, and a view of the alpine-glow on the higher mountains to the south, filled Hansen with a sense of belonging. He could think of no other place on earth that he'd rather be at that moment. It was a perfect evening.

"What do you think you'll do with the information you have on Hillby's accident," Sam asked.

"Sam, at this point I don't know. If there were anything concrete, I'd give it to the F.B.I. and step aside. I'm certainly not an investigator by trade. There is a certain amount of interest on my part, because I was associated with the Senator on a couple of occasions, and for whatever reason, I seem to be drawn toward the situation of his death."

"At this time, jurisdiction in the case is Eagle County's. We probably won't ask for F.B.I. help in solving it, at least that's the way it looks at this point. Anything you can think of, fact or even an intuitive insight, will be of interest to me and the Department, Bill. I can assure you, that anything you can give us will be properly investigated. We are used to high profile situations, and, if I may say so myself, we handle them very professionally. My staff is top drawer."

"Sam, anything I think of or come across, I'll call you immediately."

Bob slept in. Earlier, he had awakened. He was sweating heavily, and needed to pee. He found that he'd gone to bed wearing the panties and bustier that he had worn to the gig. He stayed in them after going to the bathroom. Somehow, they helped raise his confidence. The panties, especially, were soft on his skin.

He had second thoughts about going directly back to bed, and decided to shoot up first. As the rush hit he dropped back on to the sheets. Bob was tired. He wanted to sleep and sleep. The heroin made him warm, everything in his body was soothed, and he couldn't hold his eyes open, everything was wonderful again.

The last few days were busier than any week he could remember. He had two or three jobs every night. A couple were all male orgies, which Ronald told him paid very well. Bob never counted the money the guys handed him, but Ronald did and it equaled the prearranged number. For these jobs, Ronald gave him extra China White. He had serviced a lot of guys a lot of times on those two jobs. In fact after the last one, last night, his backside was a little tender. The smack would take care of that. Being high took care of everything. "Being high is where it's at."

Ronald hadn't been rough on him since that one afternoon. Most of the bruises were still blue and yellow from the beating. Bob remembered being scared that day. But Ronald had been nice to him that evening. He had even given him an extra bag of heroin when he brought him back after the job. He had told Bob, when he dropped him off at the hotel, that he had to do what Ronald said and there would be no trouble. Bob said he would.

Enna looked out for him, washed his clothes, got him ready for jobs, and made sure he stayed clean. The small rashes around his middle, on his arms and on his thighs, she thought, were his skin's sensitivity to the laundry soap she used, so she decided to change soap.

Jesus was slow in finding Hamilton's solution. Hour long, heart felt prayers were offered, sometimes twice a day. Hamilton's faith was strong; he would wait for the answer. Jesus would bring things back into proportion again. "The discipline to wait," he thought, "I must maintain my personal discipline, and wait for God's answer in God's own time." In the meantime, the scotch soothed the evenings and made the waiting more palatable.

The limo, that brought them and their gear to the hotel from the airport, was nearly broad sided twice by cars skidding through red lights in the torrential cloudbursts that seemed to follow them. The driver, who obviously had been through security driving school, did a fine job steering around both "idiots." He even apologized to Phillbroom and Charles for jinxing the car and spilling their drinks. "Why hell son," Phillbroom roared, "go ahead and drive right over the next one. It will teach him a lesson." He turned to Charles, and said, "you know, I think I've spilled nearly ten dollars worth of this fine Jack Daniels in the last three minutes. How are you doin'?"

"Harry, it looks like I'm a little behind you on that one. I'm down maybe two bucks, from the looks of my glass." He laughed.

It was apparent that the fishing trip had mellowed both men. Three days in the Louisiana bayous with fishing, campfire smoke, and a few hands of black jack, had worked it's medicine. Even the near misses in traffic failed to evoke more concern than that just discussed.

Now they were on to the second segment of the vacation, the re-entry. This part of the plan called for three days of living, more or less, out of the mainstream, but tasting bits and pieces of the French Quarter in New Orleans.

Charles had made reservations in a tiny hotel, on the edge of the Quarter, that emoted voluminous French charm. The canopy beds had lace work on the pillowcases and sheets. Every room had at least a small balcony, big enough for a small table and two chairs, where breakfast or drinks could be taken out in the open air. The rooms were filled with antiques and were spotless. The fresh flowers in desk vases were changed every day. The men were given adjoining rooms.

The afternoon was hot and very humid, following the brief cloudburst. Phillbroom elected to take a "little nap", while Charles went his own way for the afternoon. They agreed to meet up later for dinner.

Phillbroom stretched out on the bed and fell asleep immediately, even with the doors to the balcony wide open and sounds from the street falling about the room.

Charles made three calls, and then left his room after the third call. He was gone all afternoon.

When Phillbroom awakened nearly all the light was gone from the sky, and street lamps were on. His watch indicated seven minutes after eight. He reached for the phone and dialed Charles' room. "Good God almighty, I slept through the sunlight. Let me get a shower, and into some fresh clothes. I'll meet you in twenty minutes. Will supper be close by?"

"We'll be walking a couple of blocks, Harry."

"Okay, see you in a shake, I'm getting hungry."

Dinner at Antoine's was sumptuous. For Phillbroom, it started with oysters on the half shell, loaded with hot sauce.

The tall bourbon and water went to the dregs to stay up with that hot sauce. Phillbroom was flush from the quantity of pepper sauce and the quickness of the drink. Next came the crayfish bisque, followed by a tossed green salad. Another whiskey and water was sipped, about one half down, before the entree arrived, which was quail.

Charles, whose tolerance for spicy hot food was somewhat less than Phillbroom's, but wanted to stay head for head with his boss on the oysters, was on his third glass of Chardonnay when the soup course was brought to the table.

Both men were on a roll with the good times. The three days back on the bayous had set the relaxed mode of this vacation, and had enabled each to drop his guard enough to actually enjoy the immediate circumstances with a less critical eye and word. It was agreed that the stay in New Orleans would be an extension of that disposition.

Part of Charles' plan for this evening included coffee and brandies at a tiny bar a short walk away from their restaurant. Charles made a phone call on his way back from the bar's men's room. "Harry, we've done pretty well smoothing out some wrinkles these past few days. Are you game for some more wrinkle smoothing this evening?"

"It sounds to me as if you have a plan in mind."

"Some friends of mine have put together an intimate little party tonight, very discrete. Are you up for a little fun, Harry?"

"Charles, you know I'm always ready for a little fun. Tell me about this party."

"Gigi, an old acquaintance from my undergrad days at Brown, owns a large three bedroom flat a few miles from here. He and a couple of close friends get together every once in a while for a, well, let's call it a soiree. They usually invite some top quality talent, in multiples of three, of course. There's a stocked bar. And as far as I know, there are no drugs allowed. Everyone throws three to five hundred into the kitty for the talent, the bar supplies, and so forth. Gigi says everyone has a real good time. His friends are quality people who will know you only as Harry. Interested?"

"How can I say no to such a fine presentation. I will need to go back to our hotel for some more cash however."

"Don't worry about it Harry, Gigi will accept my check. Pay me back later."

"All right then, let's go to a party."

Gigi's flat, which took up the entire upper floor of the six story building, was finely outfitted with extremely modern furniture in beige and white leathers and fabrics. Walking through the off white carpet the soles of Harry's shoes disappeared in the depth of the pile. The lighting, obviously professionally done to studio quality, gave additional softness to the air-conditioned interior, and accentuated the expensive exotic sculpture and paintings in the salon.

Gigi and his friends were cordial and likable. They appeared to be around the same age as Charles, with the same level of intelligence and sophistication. Harry warmed to them immediately. The young man who had ushered he and Charles in, was now doubling as a bar tender, waiter. He asked them if they would like drinks. Two Jack Daniels and water quickly appeared.

The phone rang in the middle of an anecdotal story about a pleasure trip to Paris. The bar tender answered it, and motioned to Gigi, who took the phone briefly. The story ended with laughter all around. Gigi announced that the talent was on its way.

He also announced that this would be blind date night. "And for benefit of our guests, blind date night means that you will be provided with a bedroom and a sleep mask, and a totally tactile experience. When the talent arrives, they will each select a numbered slip of paper, from my hat, that corresponds to a number taped to the door of each bedroom, and the study. The number five will be the living room. Markus, my houseboy, has been given the night off. I will make sure the talent gets to the correct venue, and I will take the living room for myself. Gentlemen, man your quarters by reaching into my hat and selecting a lucky number. Tonight's talent is all new to us, but I'm told it's the best in the city. Off with you, and do remember you're not to remove the sleep mask until after your partner leaves in two hours.

Harry drew the master bedroom. In he went. The table lamp was the only light on. It was on the lowest setting. He guessed that he was expected to make himself ready. "What the hell," he said, stripped down, and jumped into bed pulling the sheet up around his waist, and fluffing the pillows up and sitting back against them. The anticipation was exciting. He felt the adrenalin. With a smile, he thought about the wrinkles already going away. Then he remembered the damned mask. He swung out of bed,

141

grabbed it, and got back into the same position on the bed. The mask was pulled up to his eyebrows. He understood the ploy of the mask; it heightened the senses to the touch of the anticipated sex play. "Like having tactile, old time, radio," he smiled and said aloud. Harry allowed he would go along with the game. He would pull the mask over his eyes just before his partner entered the room.

At that moment, Harry heard a quiet little knock at his door. The door opened. Down quickly came the mask. Curiosity got the best of him. He nudged the mask up just enough to see blonde hair and a very short red dress on the silhouetted figure, and then quickly pulled the corner of the mask down again. The rather disappointingly heavy voice said, quietly, "Hi, I'm Roberta. Just lay back and relax, I'll take care of everything."

Ten miles away, Hamilton staggered against his desk, reached for the chair, missed, and fell, hitting his head hard against the edge of the desk. His left arm swung out, knocked the lamp into the woven wastebasket breaking the lamp's bulb, and spinning the basket into the office drapes. The arcing filament, as it burned out, started some waste paper smoldering. The drapes were ablaze three minutes later. Hamilton was out cold. He never awakened. Nearly the whole of the second floor of the building was burning before the fire was reported. In spite of the excellent efforts of the four responding fire companies, the building was a total loss. One body was found in the debris. Hamilton's death made the front page of the morning papers.

Hansen landed the Beechcraft at Aspen. The flight from Eagle was brief, but, following his usual procedure, he topped the fuel and oil tanks, then double-checked the tie down chains, before leaving the airplane.

A quick call to the manager confirmed the prearranged rental condo, filled with antique furniture, two blocks from the center of town. He had stayed there on three previous visits.

"Assa, glass of wine at the Red Onion at five fifteen?"

"See you there!"

The ceiling camera and the camera on the far wall began silently rolling the instant the bedroom door closed. The blonde came to the head of the bed and attached the wrist restraints to Phillbroom and then to the headboard. Even in the low light the images were quite discernible and clear, Phillbroom on his back in the king sized bed receiving oral sexual stimulation. When his partner removed everything but the garter belt and hose and straddled him, facing away toward the wall camera, it became an indisputable fact that the senator was having anal sex with a man. The low light level video cameras rolled away producing nearly three-quarter of an hour of high-resolution video images.

Assa and Hansen had a light supper at the Onion then headed for Hansen's rented condo. Over hot cups of tea the two men shared the more intimate aspects of their lives that were better discussed in private. The conversation finally arrived at it's understood grand question, when Assa asked, "So Bill, what actually brought you out here? I mean, I know it is related to the Senator's death. How deeply are you connected to this situation?"

Hansen thoroughly went over the circumstances associated

with the passage of Phillbroom's Bill, including the last minute betrayal by the two Senators. He outlined the potentials of the Bill, and the impact, in Yen and dollars, it would particularly have on the people Kogi represented. "I can agree that Hillby's death may not be in any way related to what happened in D.C., but I think the potential is unquestionably there. My intuition says it probably is."

"You still haven't answered my question, Bill. What, other than the love of flying that old Beechcraft of yours, brought you way the hell out here? The conversations you've had since you got here could have been handled by telephone in a few minutes for a few dollars. What are you looking at, thirty to forty gallons of av-gas per hour for however many hours, plus oil, plus potential overhaul costs? There must be some kind of burr under your saddle for you to have spent the time and money to get here?"

"To begin with, I needed to get out of town and away from business for a few days. Satchel and I had worked damned hard to defeat the Phillbroom Bill. When the situation went upside down I guess it hit me harder than I thought. I was looking for a reason to get away, and I found it in Hillby's death." Hansen finished speaking and found himself staring into the teacup.

"Are you happy with your business?"

"I've, influenced history a bit, made some good money, made some good friends and some interesting enemies. Sometimes I think that I'd like to walk away from the intensity of the work and maybe spend the rest of my life fly fishing the Roaring Fork River." He smiled. "I guess you could say I've enjoyed what I've done."

The phone rang. "Hello, this is Bill."

"Bill, Satchel here."

"Satchel, hey, what a surprise. Is everything okay?"

"Everything is not okay. Senator Cask is dead."

"Cask dead, what happened?" Assa turned and looked at Hansen. Hansen signaled him with his index finger.

"He was shot through the heart at point blank range, and his wallet was taken. He had just come out of the bank."

"Jesus, you mean he was robbed and killed right in front of a bank?" Assa continued to stare.

"That's the way it looks to the reporter on the radio, Bill. It happened about a half hour ago."

"Did they catch the person who did it?"

"No, the guy ran off. No one got a good look at his face. At least that's what the reporter said."

"Someone must have seen him running away."

"I guess it's a little too early for straight up information on what happened. The reporter said there were police all over the place. He gave the location, but I didn't catch it. Someplace in D.C."

"I don't like it, and I don't buy it. Know what I mean Satch?"

"Loud and clear. I know a detective on the force. I'll call him in the morning and see if he can put some more details on this thing. As for right now my wife is standing in the doorway motioning me to come on. We're late for a yacht club dance.

"So, thanks for calling me on this one Satch, I'll be in touch."

"I'll call you when I have the straight scoop on Cask. Good night."

Hansen hung up the receiver and looked at Assa. "Senator Cask gunned down in D.C., now isn't that convenient?" Without waiting for the answer, he dialed a number and said, "Hello. Sheriff Goddard, please. Okay, I'll call him at home, I have the number."

It was nearly ten o'clock when Phillbroom came down for the Continental breakfast. He looked a little tired. "Excuse me Mister Phillbroom, this was left for you earlier this morning," said the desk clerk, turning to retrieve a manila envelope from the Senators room mail slot.

He took the envelope. There was no writing on it. The clasp had been bent over and the flap had been cellophane taped as well. Putting it under his arm, he walked to the coffee urn, drew a cup, added sugar and sat down at a small table next to the windows. The coffee was hot, rich and sweet, and tasted of roasted chicory.

Phillbroom slid a table knife under the flap to cut the envelope open. He pulled the first color picture only half way out before he recognized it's content. The wall camera had provided a perfect image of him on the bed, obviously straddled by a male in hose and garter belt. The picture made him sick. He felt nauseous as he quickly pushed the photo back into the envelope. The couple at the other end of the room was obviously involved in intimate conversation and had not noticed anything beyond each other. The only other person in the breakfast room was an older man, three tables away with his back to him, eating.

Phillbroom thought for a few seconds. He overcame an instant of panic, then took a sip of the coffee to take away the cotton ball dryness that had formed in his mouth. His shaking legs carried him back to the front desk. "Who delivered this," he demanded, waving the envelope at the clerk.

"Some young man in a leather jacket. He looked like a courier. Is there something wrong Mister Phillbroom?"

Phillbroom stifled his true answer and said, "No, I just wanted to give a reply." He was sure his voice might have betrayed his feelings.

"Sorry Sir. The young man said that he had a delivery for you. I took the envelope, and put it in your room box. He left without saying anything more. This was about an hour ago."

"Well, thank you," Phillbroom said, turning as he did and walking slowly to the elevator. Anger was beginning to envelope him. He hammered on the up button for the elevator until the door opened. Once inside he hammered on the floor button until the door closed and the car started up.

"That son of a bitch," he half whispered, trying desperately to control the natural volume of his voice. "That son of a bitch." Stepping from the elevator to the door to Charles' room, he wanted to put a fist through it, but with the utmost of his control, quietly knocked. There was no noise behind the door. He knocked again a little louder. Again, no noise, no response.

Philbroom dialed Charles's room from his bedside phone and let the ringing last a full minute. The photos had excellent clarity. It was easy to discern who's face was behind the mask in both pictures. In the first scene the other person's face was buried between his thighs. From the back this person certainly passes as female because of hairstyle, slight body and the female undergarments. But the second photo, with panties and brassiere removed, and facing a camera, there was no question that the person was a male. The feminine appearing face was totally unknown to Phillbroom.

The enclosed typewritten note said, "You should see the video that these were made from."

Alternating feelings of anger and dread flowed over him. This may have been a grandest of pranks, but it could lead to the end of his career in the hands of enemies. Whichever end of the scale the situation was initiated from, it was now eminently dangerous. At the moment Charles was the key. Where the hell was he?

The steaming cappuccino burned his lips on the first sip. "Damn it, don't be in such a hurry," Hansen thought. "There is plenty of time for breakfast." His absentmindedness would cause his mouth to hurt the rest of the day. The absentmindedness was at least partially caused by a question absolutely lodged in his brain. The question had come from Assa last night, namely, "Why did he come out to Colorado?"

Clearly, the cost of flying Pork Barrel across two thirds of the country was expensive. Assa was right; a few dollars in telephone long distance calls and fax could have accomplished the same thing. The answer he had given Assa was an off the cuff remark, more than an answer. Yes, it was true, he really needed a vacation. He, even more than Satchel, had worked dreadfully long hours to defeat Phillbroom's legislative bill. He was tired, physically and mentally. But that wasn't the whole answer. There was something deeper, something that wasn't very near the surface that had driven him in the decision to fly out. In retrospect, this trip did appear to have been made in haste, but that kind of decision wasn't his normal mode of operation. Right now, the answer wasn't there. So, until such time as it faded from view, this trip would be called vacation.

At the moment, he only felt half awake. He hadn't slept particularly well. And somewhere in the night, or maybe all night long, for all he knew, he had had a reoccurrence of the same dream that he'd dreamed at the beach.

She came to him out of the sun. Her loose beige dress floated to the ground, revealing a beautiful, tanned female body. Down the shaft of sunlight came the woman, one foot in front of the other. Each step primed her titillation. She had always loved him. She is going to have him now, on this beach, in this sunshine. The hibiscus flower scent flowed over him from the flowers in her hair, as she straddled him, knelt down, and through some mysterious force poured love into him. The sun was at such an angle that he could only see the outline of her face. He instinctually knew her, but couldn't see her face. He brought his hand up to shade his eyes. "Who are you," he asked? He awakened with a start.

Hansen blew on the coffee as he brought the cup to his sensitive lips, for a second sip. The proximity of the superheated rim of the cup to those sensitive lips told him that it was still too hot. He smiled again to himself. "My God, another mystery; just who the hell is this woman in the dream? I know her. If I could just see her face." The phone rang, it was Satchel. "Nothing new to report about Cask. My friend at the police department said he had heard nothing since last night. It looks to him like a straight forward case of robbery at gun point that went wrong."

"Did you say anything about our theories?"

"No. Do you think I should have?"

"When you talk to him again, tell him about what we theorize might be happening. When you come to the part about Senator Hillby's death, please don't say anything about me nosing around here in Western Colorado. As far as you or anyone in the office is concerned, I'm here on vacation."

"Actually, that's what you are doing, aren't you?"

"Roger, dodger, Satch."

"So Bill, I'll be back in touch in a day or two. Get some

rest. And don't let that Norske sheriff lead you astray."

"Thanks for your concern. Assa and I are going to be doing some heavy-duty fishing tomorrow through the weekend. The nightlife will be limited, trust me. Since I may be away from this phone, which doesn't have an answering machine, attached, I'll call you in a couple of days for an update on the Cask situation and on our business. Will evenings be a good time?"

"Evenings will be fine. Regarding business, it's actually humming right along. Everyone is happy and at work on time, etcetera. Two of our new accounts have called to say they are very pleased with the data we've supplied. And lastly, I've just about finished the information survey for Norske Fiske. I should have it in presentation form by next Wednesday."

"Sounds like you have things well in hand, Satch," Hansen said reaching for the coffee cup.

"My normal, superior management technique saves a business one more time."

"Okay Satchel, I get the picture. Don't let that back patting mess up your rotator cuff, you rascal. It could spoil your tennis."

"Talk to you on the weekend, Bill."

"Bye."

Chapter 14

"Coming Down Your Way"

There was no way that he was going to "stick his dick out again, and get it shot off," thought Schultz. The gunman had made a gigantic impression. Forget about that fax he'd sent to Kogi, there would be no "Kill The Bill" major campaign headed by one, Rendel Schultz. Life was too short, especially with some guy shooting at you. Besides, the Coalition wasn't exactly giving hazard duty pay for all the risks he had taken. Enough is enough. In the morning he would call the headquarters to tell them he had quit. Two minutes later he'd get on the road, let things cool out for a while, lay low.

Maybe he'd go up into Oregon, stay with a cousin in Eugene, or better yet, get out of the rain and fog and head for Colorado. Last year he had made friends with a young couple from Boulder and a couple of aging hippies from Aspen. They had all marched together and cluttered up some intersections with their bodies during a couple of demonstrations. Before they left to go back to Colorado, both couples told him he had a place to stay if he ever got out that way.

He was pretty sure his old rusty Datsun could make it. It looked like an abandoned car, but the engine still ran fine. Schultz was never much of a car man, the neglect was evident. The paint had begun to wash off in the rain. Instead of orange it was becoming a sort of strawberry-tan color with various rust spots adding a little mottling in places. The salt air blowing off the Bay made quick work of unprotected metal edges or areas where the paint had chipped away. In the past few years the Datsun had become a mobile billboard for the bumper stickers that littered the rear window, covered every inch of the trunk, and the bumpers, proclaiming which ever catch words the Coalition causes were employing when the sticker was printed.

He dialed the front desk, "No, Mr. Phillbroom, there have been no messages left, other than that package this morning."

"Then, can you tell me, when did Mr. Aramin go out?"

"Sorry Mr. Phillbroom, I didn't see him leave. I've been here since eight."

"Thank you," Phillbroom said and hung up. Then he told himself, " Don't panic here. Take some deep breaths. Think things through. You have to make the right decisions, everything you've got is riding on what you do next. Damn, stop loading yourself!" He poured a glass of water, walked to a chair on the balcony and sat down. His brain was a hodgepodge, a collage of pictures of events of the past few days, of Charles, of the party, of fishing, of the blonde who came through the bedroom doorway, of Charles friends, of the bedroom as viewed through the camera lens. Why were there pictures taken? Was this a normal thing with them, or did they have ulterior motives? What did they want? The only thing he knew, at this point, is that they had the pictures. What they wanted, would come next. What ever it was, he would meet it head on.

In the mean time he had to find Charles. He was the only connection to the place and the people involved. Something had to be done. He would retrace last night's movements, up until the taxi picked them up to go to Gigi's apartment. It wasn't much of a plan, but it was the best he could come up with. Perhaps he'd pick up some clue that would help him find where Charles had gone. At the moment he couldn't remember any of the taxis route. He hadn't paid much attention to it last night. By God, if Charles were involved in this his hide would get tacked to the barn door.

Bob was sick. He had shot up only a couple of hours ago with the good stuff, he knew he should be asleep still, but he felt sick to his stomach, and was sweaty, the sheets were soaked. His neck was swollen. He felt okay at work last night. It was an easy night with just one gig, an older guy. Ronald had taken him and three of the women to a party. It was an early, easy evening. He didn't start feeling bad until he got home. The smack helped but now two hours later he felt real sick. It felt like the flu. He wondered when Enna was coming. She would know what to do to make him feel better. Oh, he was so nauseated. Better lie down until he felt good enough to do another hit. There was only one packet left. Enna could fix him up, maybe get some more smack from Ronald. He would need more in just a few hours. In a state of near panic, Bob was just able to crawl to the sink where his kit and stash were, and prepare the heroin for injection. It took every bit of his energy. When it took effect there was nothing left, he couldn't crawl back to the bed. He stayed curled up on the floor, beside the sink, as he numbed going on the nod.

Enna found him there at ten that morning and got him back into bed. She didn't like what she saw. The boy was very sick. He needed a doctor. With the pay phone in the lobby, she called Ronald. Ronald was very annoyed at being called at that time of day. "Yes, yes!" He would come over.

The gleaming white Lear 23 taxied off the runway and onto the ramp, passing in front of Hansen's Beechcraft. Hansen, at the door, turned to watch the beauty scream it's way past to a parking place in front of the small terminal building. Something about it was vaguely familiar. He was intent on retrieving his fishing gear from the rear of the cabin.

"Those turbines are so damned noisy," he said to himself, glancing toward the Lear as the engines were shut down. Then it hit him. "The plane, that Lear, it's Kogi's." Hansen walked up the Beech's aisle in order to look out of the cockpit windows at the airplane. At that moment, the stairway door on the Lear was opened, and swung down. Kogi and two husky six-footers got off. All three were wearing expensive sports clothes that looked slightly out of place in the blue jean atmosphere of Western Colorado. Hansen figured that the two big guys were probably bodyguards with nine millimeter pistols hidden someplace on their body builder frames. As the baggage was being handled, by the big guys only of course, a forth person descended to the concrete apron. Hansen did a double take, it seemed incredulous. It was Charles Aramin, Phillbroom's new assistant. "What the hell is he doing flying around on Kogi's plane," Hansen asked out loud, "and what are the two of them doing here?" He just stood there, hunched over the co-pilot seat staring out at the scene.

The luggage was taken to a waiting limo by the hard bodies. Kogi stopped beside the nose of the Lear and chatted briefly with the pilot and co-pilot, then he and Charles walked to the limo and got in.

"I can't believe what I just saw," Hansen said. He moved to the rear of the plane and got out. "A little information would be handy." He gathered up the fishing gear duffel, locked the door, and headed for the Lear.

"Hi," said Hansen, looking in the portside cockpit window at the pilot and co-pilot, "I watched you guys arrive from my Beech over there. Where have you come from?"

"Well," started the pilot, in a deep Texas drawl, "we left New Orleans, made a little pit stop at Oak City, and came on in here."

"A good flight?"

"Yeah, I reckon you could call it that. No weather to speak of. No turbulence until we started letting down over Colorado Springs. Pretty hard not to call every flight in this machine good."

"She's a beauty all right. Looks new."

"Sixty hours total. A lot of that check out time."

"Is this your home base?"

"Naw, we're just here for a few days."

"Headed on back to New Orleans then, I suppose?"

"Don't know. Just where ever the boss wants to go we take him."

"Nice talking to you. I can see you need to finish your log books, so I'll leave you to it."

"Yeah, there's always paperwork. Have a good one."

Hansen walked to the rented Chevy, set the fishing stuff in the trunk and headed back into town to have a chat with Assa.

Phillbroom walked the route that he and Charles had taken the previous day. In the daylight of midmorning, and his present state of mind, things looked quite different. The restaurant was closed for another hour and a half. So he went on to the little bar where they had had brandies. It was open. The darkness of the interior took nearly a full minute to get used to. A bartender and four patrons were grouped at the other end of the bar, with storytelling in progress.

"Hi, can I get something for you," the bartender asked cordially. Phillbroom sat down on the stool nearest the entrance.

"You know, something of the alcoholic persuasion might

not be a bad idea," Phillbroom heard himself say. "How about a Bloody Mary, with some of that fancy Russian vodka."

"A great choice sir. We make our own Bloody Mary mix fresh every morning. Would you like that in a large roly-poly or a double old fashioned glass?"

"Old fashioned, please."

The bartender hand crafted the drink and poured freely from the Stoly bottle. Phillbroom, watching him work, was entertained to the point of actually forgetting, for the minute, his distress. As the drink was served, the artisan asked," Celery or okra or without?"

"I could never go wrong with okra," the Senator smiled.

Two long, pickled okra were diagonally speared and laid across the top of the glass. Two additional wedges of lime were served on the white ceramic coaster. The presentation had the look of a Gauguin still life. Phillbroom, with sheer appreciation, savored the notion, and then took a sip. It was the best he'd ever drank.

The bartender brought a small dish of warm, roasted, shelled peanuts and sat them down near the drink. Phillbroom smiled, "That is positively the best Bloody Mary I've ever been served."

"Why, thank you Sir. As I said, we do our own tomato juice daily. The owner selects each tomato that goes into it. He also has a special supplier of limes, the flavor is constant. It all helps."

"My compliments."

"Thank you," the bartender smiled.

Philbroom, who prided himself on being able to handle situations of any prominence, found it extremely difficult to collect himself at the moment. His plan, such as it was, to get to the bottom of this prank, or what ever the hell it was, was weak at best. Scenes of those photos kept interrupting his concentration, and the guilt and dread of consequences that his logic told him were soon to follow. Yes, this was far more serious than just a prank. Who put this all together? Who was out to get him? He took a long sip of the Bloody Mary.

"Gertrude? Hi it's Bill. How are things going back there?"

"Bill, hello! The business is perking right along. How's the fishing?"

"The fish are getting smarter every year. I'm a little unsure of how long I can keep masquerading as a fisherman."

"I'm sure you're doing fine. Now, what brings your thoughts back to us here in the workhouse?"

"I need to talk with Satchel. It's fairly important, Gertrude."

"You missed him by ten minutes. Can I relay anything or would you like him to try you later in the day?"

"Relay this, as soon as he gets back in. Tell him Charles, Phillbroom's new assistant, has just ridden into Aspen in

Kogi's plane, with Kogi! Ask Satch if he can get a handle on what's going on. Tell him that I spoke with the pilot who said they had just come from New Orleans."

Gertrude was stunned.

"Gertrude, are you there?"

"Yes. Yes, I was just writing this all down," she lied. Then thinking of the importance, she did write Hansen's words down. "The instant Satchel gets back in I will give this to him."

"Great. Oh, and tell him that I'll be out of my room until later in the afternoon, I'm going to nose around a little. See what I can find. You have the phone number here."

"I'll tell him," she said.

"Okay, thanks Gertrude. Talk to you later."

"Bye Bill." Gertrude hung up.

She dialed Phillbroom's office number. "Hello, Senator Phillbroom's office."

"Hello. Will you connect me with the Senator's private secretary? I believe her name is Margoty."

"One moment please."

"This is Margoty."

"Margoty, this is Gertrude Steen, I'm a friend of the

Senator. I need to contact him right away regarding a matter that is urgent and confidential."

"Ms. Steen, of course. I have the Senator's itinerary. I'll call his hotel and have him call you. Where can you be reached?"

Gertrude gave her private line number. "And please emphasize that this is urgent Margoty."

"I'll call him right away, Ms. Steen."

"Thank you."

"You are very welcome. Good bye."

Two hours later, the call rang on the private number. "Gertrude, what a delightful surprise. Margoty left word to call you. She said it was urgent. I just returned to the hotel and retrieved the message and called. Is everything all right?" His voice had a ring of stress in it.

"Harry, I know that you and Charles are supposed to be on vacation together. I just found out that Charles is in Aspen."

The phone was silent several seconds, then, he spoke. "He's in Aspen? How in the world did you come by this information?"

"Bill Hansen saw him there, at the airport."

Phillbroom cleared his throat. "Whoa up here. You're a friend of Bill Hansen? Why did he tell you about Charles?

Would you be kind enough to fill me in a little here, I seem to be missing something."

"Harry, I am Bill Hansen's office manager. Bill doesn't know that you and I have been seeing each other, by the way. He called a couple of hours ago and left the information about Charles with me to give to Satchel, his partner."

Again the phone was quiet for a few seconds. Then Phillbroom asked, "Why would Bill notice Charles?"

"Charles arrived in Aspen today in Kogi's airplane, with Kogi."

Gertrude thought she heard "Oh Christ" whispered, then silence again for several seconds. "Harry? Harry, I could pretend that I don't understand what is going on, but I'm not politically stupid. This doesn't smell too good to me. Can I be of any help to you?"

"How can I get in touch with Bill?"

She read him the phone number. "He will be at this number later in the day."

"You said that Bill is unaware that we've been seeing each other?"

"Yes."

"I guess it will come out in the open when I call. Is that going to be a problem for you, Gertrude?"

"Harry, I can honestly tell Bill that I was in contact with you to find out about Charles. It still leaves me in something of a gray area since you and Bill are opposed on 87788. But I believe Bill trusts me, and I can explain you and I to him. I don't believe he'll feel compromised."

"That's fine, then. I'll call Bill in the early evening. By the way, I had Margoty get me routed into Aspen on a flight tomorrow afternoon."

"Is there anything that I can do for you, Harry?"

"You have no idea how much you have helped with that original phone call. I do appreciate what you've done for me with that. As soon as this thing with Charles is straightened away, I'd like to see you again. After all, I need the chance to lie to you about the fish I caught."

"It's a date Harry. And I will bring the Guinness World Record Book along."

"You can't just leave him here Ronald. This boy is bad sick," said Enna.

"I ain't got the time to go messin' with this junkie. You just walk him through those hospital doors and dump him in the lobby. Someone will find him. I sure as hell don't want him tied to my tail. Just get him in there, and let's get the hell out of here. He's too fucked up to work. He is out of the loop Enna. Get rid of him. Let's roll here."

"I can't just dump him Ronald. I just can't."

"Well then, get him the fuck out of this car, I'm out of here.

And if you stay, don't go shootin' your mouth off about nothin, understand?"

"I know. I'll figure out some kind of story for the hospital. You won't be included."

"I better not be. I'm gone." The Cadillac's tires made crisp chirps as the car left the Emergency Entrance driveway.

Bob was so weak that he couldn't stand alone. He only walked because Enna held him upright. She walked him in through the Emergency Entrance double doors, and sat him in a large overstuffed chair. She went over to the admitting clerk, and said, "This young man is very, very ill. I don't know who he is or where he lives, except that he told me his name is Bob. I found him a few blocks away from here. My boyfriend and I felt sorry for him and brought him to you. I sure hope you can do something for him. He don't look good."

The admitting clerk spoke quietly and briefly to a duty nurse. The duty nurse came around the counter and walked over to Bob, checked his pulse and noticed the needle tracks up both arms. Bob remained semi-conscious and reclined in the large chair, with his eyes closed. The nurse's attention went to the enlargements on his neck, then pulled the eyelids up noticing the pin point pupils. She walked back to the admitting counter and had brief words with the clerk, who summoned two burley orderlies who brought a wheelchair. Enna quickly disappeared out the Emergency Entrance doors before any more questions could be asked.

Rendel Schultz called Monte and Myra from a roadside telephone booth in Basalt. They were genuinely happy to hear from him. He found them easily. The Victorian style two story was two blocks from Aspen town center. They were out to meet him at the gravel driveway when he drove in.

"Well Bill, looks like you've got yourself a nice little mystery here," Assa smiled.

"What in the world are Kogi and Charles doing together? And why the hell are they in Aspen?" Hansen looked astonished.

"Bill, if anyone knows that Aspen is a party town, it's you. You know the caliber of person this town draws. We have royalty. We have the super rich. We have the famous and some infamous. People come here to party, to really let their hair down in the company of their peerage. Maybe that's the evil intent of your acquaintances, to have a little fun. You know that one of Kogi's companies owns a block of condos at the base of Little Nell. He could even be popping in to have a look at his assets. As for this guy Charles, he might be just another freeloader."

"Assa, as I explained before, Charles and Kogi are on directly opposing sides of a very high and volatile political fence. What we're observing here is a very unnatural phenomena. My Washington self says political hanky-panky is afoot."

"So, my friend, what are you going to do?" asked Assa.

"I have a call into my office. Satchel will find out if any information is available, about Charles jumping ship. I'd like some reliable input before I confront anyone. Kogi's pilot said that they would be staying a few days, so I don't have to worry that they'll be blowing out of town before I can get in their faces. Hey, how about getting out to tease the trout for a couple of hours. I don't expect to hear from Satch until four or five o'clock."

Assa motioned for Hansen to "come on" as he walked toward the door, punching his radio mike switch to tell the office that he'd be out for the afternoon.

At five thirty the phone rang for nearly two full minutes before the caller hung up. One minute later Hansen unlocked the door and ambled into the condo, setting his fishing gear down in the entry closet. The phone rang a second time. "Bill here."

"Bill, it's Satchel."

"So, you got my message. Any information?"

"All I can get is that Phillbroom and Charles are on a mini vacation in and around New Orleans. Fishing first, out in a bayou, then a couple of days in the city to wash off the country. It looks strictly like R and R. There is no scuttlebutt regarding a break between the two of them. If something is going on, no one back here knows anything about it yet. From what you say it sounds like a major split has taken place. My God, Charles riding around in Kogi's plane. I don't get it. Bill, you don't suppose there's direct negotiation going on between Phillbroom and Kogi?"

"Isn't that strange, I never thought about negotiation, only hanky-panky. Shows how my mind works, I suppose."

"Has Phillbroom talked to you yet?"

"Phillbroom? No, I haven't talked to Phillbroom."

"Well, you will. Gertrude was able to get hold of him in New Orleans. She said that he'd be calling you this afternoon."

"Good for Gertrude. She does get things done. Are we paying her enough?"

"Bill, she makes well above the average for her position in D.C., in fact, she is..."

"Hold it Satch. Hold it. I was only approving her actions, and giving your CPA chain a little tug."

"Of course, I knew that."

"Okay Satch, thanks to you and Gertrude for the intel report. I'm eager to hear what Phillbroom has to say. It's an interesting development. Anything more on the killing of Senator Cask?"

"Nothing. My contact in Homicide says there are almost no leads. The only real thing the police have recovered is a nine-millimeter bullet. It's being tested to see if the blood and stuff on it belong to Cask. They still don't have any witnesses that can give an indent on the perpetrator. Anything new on Hillby's death?"

"Sheriff Goddard is playing pretty close to the chest on it. I think it's safe to say however, that the investigation is continuing."

"Sometimes I think we think police work is like what they show on TV, and that everything is solvable in a one hour time frame."

"Your right on with that, Satch," Hansen laughed.

"Okay, I'm ringing off now. Let me know what Phillbroom has to say after this phone conversation takes place. I'll be home later."

"I'll call you tonight Satchel."

"Thanks Bill."

Ten minutes later the phone rang again. It was Phillbroom. "Bill, I'm happy to have caught you in."

"Harry, thank you for calling me. I know that Gertrude was able to track you down. And I know that she probably gave you the news about Charles and Kogi. And I hope you'll forgive me for sticking my nose in, perhaps where it doesn't belong."

"You can't know how much help you've been to me. I know you don't owe me a thing Billy, but I would be obliged if you can give me a little bit more of your assistance with respect to this Charles-Kogi matter?"

"Harry, how can I help?"

"I am scheduled to arrive at Aspen, on Aspen Airways at four fifteen tomorrow afternoon. Can you meet me?"

"Of course."

"That will be fine. And I want this to be a confidential visit, there's a sensitive situation that's involved here. Does Charles or Kogi know you saw them, or did they see you?"

"No. I am reasonably sure that they don't know I'm in town."

"Good. I would appreciate it if it could be kept that way. I'll fill you in when I see you."

"Are you sure that you don't want some kind of security set up at the airport, or while you're in town? And will you need a place to stay."

"I want to quietly get into town without any fuss that would alert Kogi or Charles. Being a small town, people will know soon enough that I'm there. I need to be able to visit with Charles before word gets around. And Margoty set me in a suite at the Hotel Jerome, under the name of Jones. Can you believe that?"

"Jones, huh? Nice disguise Harry. How will I recognize you at the airport?"

"I'll be the one in an old fishing hat," Phillbroom laughed.

"Okay Mister Jones, see you tomorrow afternoon at four fifteen. Understand you'll be wearing an old fishing hat."

"You have it cold, Bill. Thank you."

"You've driven a long way. You must be exhausted Rendel." She said. "We didn't mean to destroy you the first night in town. Your room is ready for you if you'd like to lie down for a while."

"Whoa, shit!" Schultz knocked the dinning room chair over as he got up from the table. "That wine gets to you at this altitude, doesn't it?"

Myra quickly came around the table and set the chair upright, checking it for damage as she did. "Are you okay, Rendel?" It was apparent that he was drunk.

"Just a little shitfaced, Myra." He staggered to the sofa and fell into a corner cushion.

Monte called from his place at the table, "Rendel, let me help you up the stairs."

Schultz couldn't quite get his eyes to focus. "Yeah, that's probably a good idea."

Monte got him up from the sofa and maneuvered the stairs, down the short hall and into the spare bedroom. "There you are my friend, a little rest and you'll be ready to kick ass."

"Talk to you later," Schultz said, dropping onto the bed and closing his eyes.

"Poor guy really got nailed by the zinfandel," Monte said to Myra after coming back down stairs.

"He did drink a whole bottle by himself, Monte. There was bound to be some kind of reaction, especially after having just come up from sea level. We're lucky he isn't sick. But then, of course, the night isn't over. In the future we're going to have to slow him up. My God, it's only eight o'clock."

"Assa, I am really not comfortable with a senator of the United States of America wandering around without some kind of security," Hansen said.

"Well, I don't have a lot of unspoken for budget, but I could change some patrol timings to coincide with Phillbroom's arrival at the airport. Are you expecting a problem?"

"No, I don't expect anything. And he is supposed to come in here very low key, but the whole of America and half the world must recognize his face. In view of the circumstances of this visit I'd appreciate someone who could interject himself into a situation if one came up."

"Have you talked to the Aspen Police Department?"

"Not yet."

"The new police chief, Sam Baxter, is a super guy and a fine law enforcement person. He also deals with this sort of high profile stuff on a daily basis. I'm sure he can be of help to you. And since most of the Senator's movements will be within Aspen City Limits, that's his jurisdiction. Beyond that, I might recommend hiring security, if it would make you comfortable. Or I can see if any of my people want to take on side work as bodyguards, unofficially, of course."

"Well, I'll have a chat with Chief Baxter in the morning."

"That's probably the best course Bill. He has people in plainclothes who can fit into any place without being obtrusive. And they're used to high profile people. Hell, it's

SOP in this town all the time."

Kogi moved to the bar and poured half a bottle of Perrier into an iced glass for himself. "Charles, you've done quite well with this assignment. So well, in fact, that I hated to take you out of Phillbroom's confidence. Would you care for a new assignment in Europe or Asia, perhaps the Malay peninsula next?"

"Mister Kogi the acceptance of an assignment venue depends on many things. Naturally I want to keep the quality of life in an acceptable range. I certainly prefer city to country life. I am an urban person. Intellectual stimulation has never been a problem with an assignment you've given me," with this he gave Kogi a little half smile. Kogi replied with a half smile of his own.

"Naturally I would like to keep you here, in the States Charles, however as we've already discussed, the good Senator will soon be on your trail in person or electronically, and I do believe he will act unkindly toward you should he find you. The companies I represent would welcome you with open arms to a position of your choice from a number of high-level selections. Knowing your tastes, I might suggest a Paris assignment that will soon be available. There is also a situation taking place in Prague that a man of your talents would find interesting. I know we have something that you'll respond to favorably."

"Really, my immediate concern, after off loading the New Orleans video to you, is to get as far away from the Senator's area of influence, as soon as possible, and definitely before you make whatever use you're planning to make of that video."

"Take advantage of this condominium for as many days as you like. It's at your disposal, Charles. You are my guest. We have the best security, food, drink, accommodations, and a choice of excellent companionship if you so desire. We have access to the best of the best of Aspen's charming provisions. As you've no doubt noticed, you're half a block from the center of the nightlife. "

"Are you inferring that you aren't planning to stay long?"

"My plans include three days here in Aspen, then to Los Angeles for a week, before returning to D.C."

"As long as you're here in Aspen, I'll accept your hospitality. My intuition says I should get out of the U.S. soon, Mister Kogi."

"So, you will be my guest, excellent. I'll have security provide you with a key card. And, please, just call me Kogi."

"Okay, Kogi it is. Now, about the video, when do you want it?"

"You told me that you have it with you. I assumed that you are carrying it in your briefcase. I further assume that the briefcase is locked."

"Correct on both assumptions, Kogi."

"Is it also correct that you are due a bonus for this video?" Kogi smiled.

"Correct, a third time," Charles returned the smile.

"And how would you like payment made?"

"In view of my present need for flexibility, let's say fifty thousand cash and the balance transferred into my Swiss account."

"Easily done Charles. Tomorrow afternoon we will make the exchange." Kogi lifted his glass in salute, as did Charles.

Hansen began his day, wading and casting on the Roaring Fork River. Making rolling casts, he placed his best Royal Coachman dry fly just above a deep pool formed by a large round boulder on the far bank. The fly, caught by the water flow in a circular motion, swirled around the boulder into a near placid portion of the pool. There was a silver flash in the water that erupted in a cold, snow melt volcano around the Coachman as the rainbow nailed it hard, coming completely airborne before splashing back into the pool. Hansen's reel sang in tenor as the line played out while the fish headed for the deepest part of the riverbed.

This fish was a grand master at water acrobatics. And it was apparent that the hook was in the jaw and not swallowed deeply as he twisted and rolled to get rid of it. He spun from the pool and headed upriver. Hansen slowly slogged along after him, feeling his way on the rocky bottom. The line continued to fly off the reel as the rainbow accelerated in center stream. Hansen's left foot came down on a very large, mossy rock. He felt himself slowly loosing balance. Down he went, in very slow motion. The icy water poured into his waders filling them chest high as he slid off the rock into a deeper part of the river.

With a gallant isometric maneuver he managed to touch bottom in an upright position, with his fly rod still solidly in his right hand. The left hand clung to his trusty panama hat. The sunglasses tenderly balanced themselves halfway down his nose. Line stopped being dragged off the reel. Clearly this damned fish was up to something.

Standing chest deep with the waders no longer buoyant, but now laden with river, his footing was quite secure. Full attention was on fishing. He hauled in line and hit the spool take up lever. The reel ground in alto and the line grew taunt again, but it felt different. "I think it's wound around a rock," Hansen said to himself. Trying everything he could think of to dislodge the line, he slowly began edging toward the near shore.

No tugging or whipping of the line produced any positive results. As Hansen came up on to the riverbank he decided it was time to bite the bullet. Aligning the eyes of pole with the spot in the water where the floating line went in, and a hank of line wound round his hand, he slowly backed up. The line got guitar string taunt, and then went slack. He reeled it in.

To his great surprise, Hansen got back all of his tapered floating line, and the entire leader to where the Royal Coachman had been tied. He would have bet a hundred dollars that after winding the line around a rock the trout had backed out of the hook and left it to get caught and broken off when the line was pulled between adjoining rocks. Mister Rainbow now had a sore mouth and was mad as hell with himself for having fallen for the same old dirty trick. "My God, a Royal Coachman again, I can't believe I did that."

Jerry Tiff

"Nurse, nurse."

"Just a moment Mrs. Bradley." The duty nurse stopped Bob's wheelchair just beyond the doorway to the second examining room, and patted Bob on the shoulder. "I need to stop here for just a second." She went into the examining room and said, "The doctor will be with you very shortly, Mrs. Bradley. Please be patient. Just a couple minutes more."

Bob slumped in the chair, his head rolled forward onto his chest.

"Well, why is he taking so long?" Asked Mrs. Bradley.

"He's with the very sick little girl who just came in."

"Well, I'm sick too," said Mrs. Bradley, and began to sob loudly.

Bob's arms slipped off the armrests and hung down over the top of the wheels.

"Now please, Mrs. Bradley, don't upset yourself. You're going to be all right." The nurse handed her a small box of tissue. "Here we are, have a nice big blow. You'll feel better." Mrs. Bradley gave a huge honk into the two ply tissue.

At that precise moment, Bob slowly rolled forward, and then pitched out of the chair into a heap on the tiled floor in front of the wheelchair.

"Let me get the patient in the wheelchair situated, and I'll

176

be back in to check on you," said the nurse, as she backed out of the doorway.

There was Bob, on the floor, in front of the wheelchair. "Oh my God," she said as she hurried around to him. There was no sign of life.

"How about a hike up into the Maroon Bells," Myra asked. Schultz, who had slept nearly fifteen hours, came downstairs from his bedroom to the dinning table where Myra was perusing the newspaper and sipping coffee.

"Hey Myra, let me wake up a bit. Any more coffee around?"

"Sit down Rendel. I'll get you some. What do you take in it?"

"Just a touch of sugar."

She brought a large mug of coffee along with a plate of muffins. "What can I get you for breakfast?"

"To tell the truth, Myra, I think I'll see how I get along with just the coffee first. Where's Monte?"

"He'll be out for a couple of hours. He had to take our car in for some work. The appointment had been made before we knew you were going to be here, sorry."

"Hey, no problem."

"How are you feeling this morning?"

"I actually feel pretty good. Guess I should after all that sleep. Did I embarrass myself?"

"Well, you did get a little drunk. Do you remember Monte getting you up the stairs?"

"Sort of. Last night is a little fuzzy, but the last thing I do remember is thinking about how great your tits looked in that white sweater."

"Rendel!"

"Well, that's what I remember. I didn't grab them did I," his face was between a leer and a smirk, Myra couldn't decide which."

"Rendel, fortunately you were too smashed to really get hold of anything, except maybe the bed later when it started whirling around. And it's a damned good thing you didn't try anything with me."

"You trying to tell me you don't like having them touched."

"Oh, I like having them touched all right, but I decide by whom and when and how much. Comprende?"

"I guess I'm misbehaving huh?"

"You are getting pretty close to the line."

"And if I step over it?"

"You don't want to find out Rendel. Now, why don't we

consider a little outdoor activity to get your body sweating, and your mind clear? It will also help you to acclimate. We'll take it easy."

"Is Monte coming along?"

"He's in Glenwood with the car, as I've explained, but he'll be meeting us here for supper. You are going to have to put up with me and my girlfriend Trudy dragging you through the forests."

"Trudy?"

"Yes, Trudy. She's Swiss, lives in Gstaad. She's here for the summer. You'll like her instantly."

"She has good tits?"

"If you don't behave yourself, you will be without the pleasure of my company, as well as Trudy's, and you could find yourself and your baggage on the street."

"You play rough."

"Who's playing?"

Hansen sloshed back to the rented car to get dry clothes. Fortunately there was a pair of tennis shorts, and socks in an overnight bag that he kept in the car. He quickly exchanged them for the wet khakis and boot socks. His shirt steamed as it lay on the hot hood of the car. The waders were turned inside out and placed across the windshield. In an hour everything would be dry enough to put back on. The time might be well spent trying to figure the situation with Phillbroom and Charles.

He found a large flat boulder and sat down, then an even better idea came to him. He laid down on it. Its stored warmth baked away the cold from the river. He pulled his panama hat down over his face. The sun melted away any desire to hurry back to work the river. The warmth over came him. There was no focusing on Phillbroom, only the warmth. He drowsed off.

She came to him out of the sun. Her loose beige dress floated to the ground, revealing a beautiful tanned female body as she stepped slowly down the shaft of golden sunlight, one foot in front of the other. Each step toward him primed her titillation. She had always loved him. She had always wanted him, and now she was going to have him in this sunshine, this very moment. The scent of hibiscus flowed over him from the flowers in her hair as she stood over him and looked down, wordlessly transmitting love and lust. The sun was in his eyes. He knew her, but couldn't make out her face. "Who are you," he asked? Hansen awakened with a start.

The Panama hat, so carefully placed over his face, had fallen onto the ground beside the boulder. The sun rested fully on his face, his body was wet again, but this time with sweat. The dream, as it always did, blurred reality. It took several moments to totally awaken and come out of it. The woman and the situation were spell binding. Hansen grabbed his hat to shade his eyes and looked at his watch. "My God, I've been out for an hour. I need to think about getting back to town. I want to get cleaned up before collecting Harry at the airport," he said to himself, without getting up from the face of the boulder. "She is so real.

Why is this dream repeating itself?" He lay there thinking about the dream and the woman, trying to analyze the reason for the reoccurrence. But he was relaxed and the high-altitude sun started its work again, soon his alpha-state became another full-blown nap.

Phillbroom walked from the turboprop to the small terminal building. Once inside, he turned on his famous 'good old boy' grin for Hansen, but Hansen wasn't there. "If this is what Billy Hansen considers a low-key approach, he's exceeded my wildest expectations," he said to himself. The smile faded. He walked over to Aspen Airways counter, and eased in beside a young woman whose ticket was being typed on the computer. "Excuse me Mam," he said to the young woman, his best fatherly smile brushed on his face. And then to the ticket agent, he said, "I'm a passenger who just came in. Where would I inquire about messages that may have been left for me?"

"I can help you sir," said the attractive female doing the typing, "I'll be with you in half a minute." She made brief eye contact with him, giving credibility to her answer.

"Thank you mam," he said to the ticket agent. And to the young woman he said, "Sorry to have butted in."

She looked up, and said, "No problem."

Phillbroom was about to engage her in more small talk when he saw what he thought was Hansen's face appear under a tan panama hat in a group of people coming in the door from the street. As the man came in he was dressed in a wrinkled long sleeved chambray shirt with the tail out over a pair of white tennis shorts. Phillbroom was unsure that it actually was Hansen. He had never seen him without a dark blue suit and an expensive tie. The sunglasses came off. It was Bill Hansen all right.

"Hey Billy."

"Mr. Jones, I am so damned sorry I'm late. I'll explain later. "Phillbroom smiled, and said quietly, "I thought I was the one who was going to appear low key. Son, that's quite a getup. I like it." He slapped Hansen on the back.

"Harry, I fell in when I was fishing this morning, and didn't get back to town in time to change."

"I suppose the fish got away too," Phillbroom chided.

"Yeah, I guess he did." Hansen shook his head.

They started to walk outside as the ticket agent waved, "Sir, I can help you now."

"No need, my ride showed up. But thank you anyway for your courtesy."

"I really don't understand what you're so pissed off about, Myra," Shultz said, rubbing his face where she had just slapped it.

"You are such a piece of shit Rendel. All day long you have been a total asshole. You can't keep your dirty hands off Trudy. And you were told, but didn't pay any attention. We take you to one of the most beautiful places in Colorado, and what do you do? You get half in the bag from rum in a hip flask you're carrying. You ruined what should have been a wonderful afternoon, and you have embarrassed me."

"It wasn't rum, it was rye whisky. And you're jealous because I made a pass at your girlfriend instead of you," Schultz said with a half smile, still rubbing his cheek.

"Well aren't you too cute Rendel. You are out of here, buster." She walked into the house and slammed the door behind her before Schultz could enter.

Schultz gently rapped on the door. "Come on Myra, admit it, you're jealous," he giggled.

A second floor window was opened. Five seconds later the first of Schultz possessions was thrown through the opening.

Schultz looked up with boozy instability. "What the fuck are you doing?"

A sleeping bag, still rolled up, and a rucksack flew into space next. "You are out of this house Rendel, and you will never be welcome back. I know a lot of people in this town, word will get around very fast about you. You would do well to get the hell out of Aspen, now."

"But Myra, this isn't that big a thing."

"Pick up your shit, load it in that piece of shit, pig sty car of yours and get the fuck out of my driveway. You have one minute before I call the police." And she slammed the window closed.

Schultz yelled back at the closed window, "You're the piece of shit Myra. You're the total asshole, you bitch, you low class rotten fuck." Schultz angrily started picking up his stuff, and threw it into his car's back seat. "You haven't heard the last of this you bitch," he yelled, as he got behind the steering wheel. Spinning the rear wheels and slinging gravel from the driveway, he gunned his car out onto the street in reverse.

"Charles, keep the tape in the briefcase and bring it with you," said Kogi.

"What's up?"

"We're taking it to a studio a couple of blocks away to be reproduced. In fact, if you would like a copy I'll have one made for you."

"That's not necessary Kogi. As I've said, traveling light will be my by-word for a while, with no excess baggage. For me the tape has no meaning, it was only a job. Phillbroom was just a target. I have no bones to pick with the man, other than staying out of his sight."

"As you wish. Shall we get underway?"

"Indeed." Charles picked up the briefcase and followed Kogi to the door. At the door to the courtyard, Kogi signaled his two bodyguards who fell in behind he and Charles as they left the condo entrance.

Crossing the bridge into town, Phillbroom, who had kept to small talk until now, said, "Bill this situation with Charles is not a good one. I believe he is, for some reason totally unknown to me, out to discredit my personal life. He disappeared from sight in New Orleans after a night on the town. When Gertrude called telling me that you had seen him in Aspen, I felt a certain amount of relief for his welfare. When she said you'd seen him with Kogi, my blood ran cold. I have to confront Charles face to face. That's my sole reason for being here. Besides, the altitude up here kicks my backsides," he added, his sense of humor apparently returning.

"Finding out where he's staying, and if he's staying with Kogi, should be easy enough. Kogi's company owns a group of condos near the center of town. When do you want to start?"

"Now would be fine."

"You don't want to go to your room first?"

"Bill, this situation needs immediate attention. Let's go find Charles."

"Okay. Let's start looking for Charles at Kogi's condos. They are just a few blocks away. Maybe we'll get lucky and find a parking place nearby. Aspen is as bad as D.C. or San Francisco to find parking in these days. Incidentally, do I stay in the car or go in with you."

"I really don't expect a difficult confrontation with him, if that's what you're asking, Bill."

"I guess that was what I was asking. Actually, what I'm really asking is do you want the police handy, just in case?"

"My Lord no. I don't want police involved in this."

"Are you absolutely sure?"

"I couldn't be more sure my boy. And I do not expect trouble, only a little healthy intellectual stimulation."

"If it should go beyond that, do I have your permission to bring in the cops if it's necessary to save your non-intellectual backsides?"

"Billy I'm not going to let this thing get to anywhere near that kind of a situation. I don't want police, or police reports, or reporters, or publicity. I plan to act accordingly. Satisfied?"

"Guess I'll have to be Harry."

Phillbroom did a double take, the rapidly said, "Stop the car Bill."

"What, why?"

"Billy, stop the Goddamned car, now. I see him." Phillbroom was staring at a group of men on the sidewalk a hundred feet ahead. "Let me out before I loose sight of him."

Hansen brought the car close to the parked cars on his right and turned on the hazard lights. Phillbroom was out the door before the car came to a stop. The car behind Hansen also came to a stop with its hazard lights blinking, obviously unable to pass because of traffic. A third car was added to the chain. Hansen eyed them in the rearview mirror expecting horns at any second, while Phillbroom took off at a trot down the sidewalk. Hansen slowly moved ahead while trying to watch traffic and keep Phillbroom in sight.

Phillbroom got within twenty feet of Charles and felt a shortness of breath. He yelled, "Charles, Charles. Hold up a second. I need to talk with you."

Charles and Kogi turned at the recognition. Charles face noticeably tensed. He drew the briefcase tighter to his chest. Kogi shoved Charles ahead, then motioned his bodyguards toward Phillbroom. Charles, and Kogi started trotting, then running down the sidewalk. Phillbroom was now yelling louder and with heated anger, "Charles, stop, stop. I want an explanation from you, son." He started into a trot that ended in the strong arms of the two bodyguards. Charles and Kogi were running at full speed. They came to the intersection, and without hesitation ran out diagonally toward the other side of the street.

Two men in the second car behind Hansen jumped out of their car and started running toward Phillbroom. Hansen was out of his car and twenty paces behind the two men.

"That lousy asshole of a broad is ordering me out of town, well fuck her," said Schultz, as his tired old car gave up rubber when he rammed the shifter into second gear and accelerated to that gears maximum speed. The engine screamed to be shifted into the next gear as he plunged into the intersection at forty-five miles an hour.

Schultz caught the first runner with the left front fender and flung him up and over the car. He landed with his head at an odd angle. The case he was carrying went down under the left side wheels.

The second runner was hit by the right front fender and went down under the car. The car went over him and dragged him through the intersection.

Schultz cranked the steering wheel hard left out of instinct. The car went into the curb, the right wheels catching on the curb itself, flipping the machine onto its roof. Schultz was thrown out as the car went over.

The car that had been immediately in back of Hansen's Chevy spun its wheels as it went around Hansen, and stopped at the intersection's crosswalk. The two men in it got out and ran to the downed pedestrians. Both men were in jeans and sport shirts, but flashed shinny badges at their belts as they ran from their car. One produced a radio and was talking as he ran. Seconds later the wail of a siren could be heard, then two, then three. The first to the scene were the fire department paramedics, then ambulances, and then uniformed police officers who moved the crowd back to the crosswalks, at the intersection.

The men from the second car in back of Hansen had reached Phillbroom and the bodyguards at the same moment the screaming car and the two thumps were heard. All five men stood with their mouths open with horror. "Oh, Christ," one said, "he just ran right into them. He must have been doing sixty." One of the bodyguards said to the other, "Mister Kogi is down." The other bodyguard said, "Yeah, he ran right in front of the car."

Then Phillbroom was pulled away from the bodyguards and

kept protectively between the two men who identified themselves as Aspen Police. Hansen identified himself to the two plain-clothes men. The bodyguards rushed to Kogi, but were told to stay back as the plain-clothes officer at the scene checked for vital signs.

While the three accident victims were loaded into ambulances, one of the uniformed officers picked up the crushed briefcase and set it next to the curb, unsure of it's involvement in the scene. Phillbroom remembered that Charles was carrying something as he was running away. It had to be that case.

As the possibility of an incident between Phillbroom and the two bodyguards had ended, the police officers relaxed. Phillbroom excused himself on the pretext of going to check on something. He worked his way through the large group of people that had gathered around the intersection, walked straight to the briefcase, picked it up, then disappeared somewhere in back of the crowd. When he reappeared, he was carrying the briefcase, it's top slightly ajar. There was a relaxed smile on his face. He dropped the brief case back in the place it had been, walked to where Hansen was standing and said, "Before we go to the hospital, I'll stand you to a large cold martini at the nearest bar."

Sixty seconds later, as they were waiting for the double Bombay on the rocks, and the diet coke to arrive, Phillbroom turned to Hansen and said, "In the event that there is an inquiry, we need to be on the same page. I hope you'll agree that what has taken place is as follows. Charles and I were here in Aspen at the request of Mister Kogi. You, of course don't know what negotiations were transpiring but it may have had something to do with Senate Bill 87788. I had called you to pick me up at the airport, because I wanted to pick your brain about Kogi's current position on my bill. When Kogi and Charles ran from me it was because Kogi or his people got overly security cautious when they heard me shouting. That's it. What do you think? Can you live with that?"

"Funny, that's almost the conclusion my sheriff friend came to before you got here."

"Billy, I thought you were going to keep my visit confidential."

"Harry, I said I'd keep it quiet, not confidential. I wanted my friends opinion about your personal security."

"The two plain clothes boys who pulled the gorillas off me got there mighty quick. They must have been pretty close at hand."

"That must have been the hand work of my friend Assa, the sheriff, in cooperation with the town police."

"I sure hated to see Charles and Kogi cut down like that. That driver must have been out of his mind. Maybe we should get to the hospital. Truthfully, I'll be surprised if any of the three survived," said Phillbroom.

The ER doctor took Phillbroom and Hansen aside in the hallway. "Our police chief asked me to cooperate with you. However, understand that until we can notify the next of kin, this information is in the strictest confidence."

Both Phillbroom and Hansen nodded and said yes.

"The driver, Mister Schultz, is in critical condition, with some head injuries, and internal bleeding. At the moment he's in a coma. I don't believe his prospects are very good.

The younger pedestrian, Mister Aramin, was dead on arrival at the hospital. He probably died from a broken neck. There will be an autopsy.

The other pedestrian, a Mr. Kogi passed away just a few minutes ago. Heart failure with some complications appears to be the cause. Naturally there will be an autopsy as well.

At the moment, gentlemen, that's what we have. It certainly is not a very pleasant situation. These traffic accidents are a rarity of course. If you've no questions, I really need to get to work."

Phillbroom and Hansen thanked him, then walked back out through the emergency entrance.

"Poor Charles, he had a brilliant future in politics," Phillbroom said, "The boy had a lot of smarts, a lot of smarts. It's funny how things happen, isn't it? All that promise, and in an instant, nothing. As for Kogi, I never really knew him very well. But I can appreciate that he was a strong opponent."

Hansen didn't say anything until they were seated in his car. He turned to Phillbroom and said, "Harry, just what the hell is this all about? I heard what you said to Charles as he was running away. Level with me Harry."

Phillbroom thought for a second then said, with a small smile, "Well, I think we'll consider the scenario we both agreed on to be fact, and let it go at that."

"Harry!"

"Fact, Billy, fact. Now how about giving me a lift back to the airport. I think I can still catch the last flight out tonight."

"Damn Harry, where do you get the stamina? Where do you get the energy? You've only been in town for about two hours. Don't you want to rest or get a meal or something? You must be tired after traveling most of the day to get here, not to mention what happened after you arrived."

"I'm still running along okay. But, if I stop too long I'm done for. So I'd better keep moving. And besides, the altitude here doesn't agree with me. Denver is a little better. And I'll bet I can find a red eye, at that big ugly airport, that will take me back to the District of Columbia and sea level."

Chapter 15

"Midnight Sun"

"Assa, It's time to get up. It's time to go fishing." Hansen was always bright as a bulb in the morning.

"Oh God, I can't. I have a relative coming in from Norway this morning."

"Bring him along. He must fish if he's from Norway."

"It's a she, and I don't recall if she still fishes. But, you know that's not a bad idea. I don't know of anyone in Norway who doesn't like the outdoors. On top of that, she is coming from a week in New York and a weekend in Chicago. An easy day in the country with a nice picnic lunch would probably be welcomed."

"Who's making the picnic lunch? Not you, I hope?"

"My liverwurst, onion, and anchovy sandwiches are world famous, Bill. But I think I'll call The Delice and have them put something together."

"A wonderful choice Assa, and if I'm still invited along, I'll pick up half the tab. My vote is for something with smoked salmon."

"You are on for half the tab Bill. I'll pass along your request when I call. At the moment, I'm fixing a little breakfast. Do you want to come over?"

"Thanks, but I've already eaten. Why don't you stop by for me en route to the airport?"

"That will work for me. How does ten-thirty sound?"

"Terrific. That will give me time to do some fixing on my second fly pole. Your female family member can use it. By the by, who is this relative?"

"She is my older sister's oldest daughter."

"God Assa, your niece, and you make her sound Gothic. How old is she?"

"The last time I saw her was ten years ago. She was married then to a Norwegian fighter pilot who was killed while flying a NATO exercise. She must be mid to late-thirties by now. She was a family favorite, very bright with a great sense of humor. I used to tease her by calling her Marilyn, but her name is Lisa."

"Scandinavian humor huh? Why did you call her Marilyn if

her name was Lisa?"

"Marilyn, as in Marilyn Monroe, William. When she was young she was a dead ringer for the movie star except her hair was golden blonde. The guys used to go nuts. She was married to Arnie for three or four years before he was killed. Never re-married."

"Assa, I don't do setup's."

"Bill, this is not a setup. You asked, I'm just giving you a little background. Remember, old boy, she is coming out to see me, the tottering old uncle."

"Does this woman speak any English?"

"At one time she spoke it well enough to get a Masters degree from U.C.L.A. She probably remembers a little, enough to carry on a conversation with you anyway."

"Good one Assa. I deserved that."

"Yes you did, and do. I'll see you at ten-thirty. Her plane arrives at eleven."

Assa showed his badge and credentials to the security people who all knew him by face. He motioned for Hansen to follow him out to the ramp. As the left propeller came to a stop, the cabin door opened and the stairway extended. Assa and Hansen moved to the base of the stairway.

She moved out into the sunlight. Hansen gave a sudden exhale. His jaw dropped. "It's her. My God, it's her," he said in a loud whisper. She came down the stairs with the sun backlighting her face, one foot carefully in front of the other, rhythmically floating down toward him. A loose beige dress revealed a beautiful, tanned, female body. It was her, the same shape and movement that had been burned into his memory from the dream encounters, so many times. She came closer, her smile, her eyes, and at last her complete face came into focus. She was exquisitely beautiful. Hansen felt his knees weakening.

At the last step, Assa reached out and took her by the waist, and whirled her around and down onto the ramp surface. Their happy laughter filled the air as they held and hugged each other and spoke in Norwegian. Their smiles radiated to the other deplaning passengers causing them to beam as well.

Hansen collected himself, his own smile returned. Assa and Lisa turned toward him, and Assa introduced them. "Bill, this is my dear niece, Lisa." Lisa unwrapped her arms from Assa's shoulders, took a step, offering her hand. She glowed with Nordic beauty. Her deep blue eyes poured her warmth into Bill's. The scent of hibiscus swept over him. "Lisa, this is my dear friend Bill."

Bill took her hand, and held it without shaking it. He felt his face flush. There was recognition. He could feel it, coming from her, through their touch. "I am very pleased to meet you, Lisa."

"And I am very pleased to meet you," she said, looking deeply and knowingly into his eyes, "Haven't we met before, perhaps on a beach or ---maybe in a dream!" She laughed.

THE END

Printed in the United States
97724LV00002B/94-99/A

9 781432 708870